The Making of a Sailor

The Making of a Sailor

Jon Adams

Slack Water Press

Slack Water Press, Mill Valley 94941

ISBN 978-0-9797613-9-3

A Green Book: The paper used in this publication meets
standards for sustainable forestry.

for Lucy and Maja

"A sailor comes aft to take mate's place, cabin-boy goes for'ard to take sailor's place, and you take the cabin-boy's place, sign the articles for the cruise, twenty dollars per month and found. Now what do you say? And mind you, it's for your own soul's sake. It will be the making of you."

Jack London, *The Sea-Wolf*

Contents

Seaman

THERE IS NO LIGHT in the forepeak of the schooner and the air is heavy with the smell of old canvas and turpentine. The schooner pitches into a wave and the girl falls back against the hatch to the chain locker. She half-stands and pulls a coil of rope out from under her and holds it up. The smell of fresh hemp. On deck the sails shiver and the staysail-sheet slides across the horse, metal scraping on metal. There's another smell, coming from the chain locker, saltwater and estuary mud. The schooner pitches again and seawater bursts over the bow and washes across the deck above. In the lull the girl listens for the foghorn on the lightship. There it is, far off. And then another blast, very loud. That's the schooner's fog horn. She can come out of the forepeak now. They won't turn back, not in this weather. She runs her hand through her hair. Is it short enough? She takes her kit bag from her lap and pulls out a watch cap and puts it on and then sets the bag in the corner, leans back and closes her eyes.

She blinks. A light is on. She sits up as the schooner rolls to port and slides down a wave. They've changed course. She blinks again as a man grabs her arm. "What are you doin' here, huh? Wait 'til the captain sees this. He's gonna feed you to the fishes." He jerks her out of the forepeak.

"Wait." The girl reaches back for her kit bag before the man pulls her into the forecastle. A man lying in the port bunk sits up. "Goddamn it, Jeff, turn the goddamn light off." He kicks his blanket into place and turns away from the light.

The man holding the girl stops. "Look what I found, Sully, a boy hiding in the forepeak." No answer. They start again, going through the door to the saloon, the man leading her by the arm. The schooner rolls to starboard and she falls against the settee. Someone in the upper bunk smells of fried grease. They go past the galley and up the midships hatch to the deck. She looks up at the mainsail, pale in the moonless night. A wave catches the stern and the schooner rolls to port. For a moment the staysail blankets the jib and the jib flaps once, then a sharp snap as it fills again. The man leads the girl aft along the weather deck. "Hey Marlin, look what I found. This little fool hiding in the forepeak."

Marlin, a shadow with a pale beard, watches them approach. "A stowaway."

"Yeah, a stowaway. Wait 'til the captain sees him. He's gonna have a fit."

Blackborne climbs out of the aft hatch. "What's this yelling about?" He looms over the three of them, Marlin at the helm, the man holding the girl's arm, and then the girl. "How old are you?"

"Eighteen, sir." Her voice low. She practiced that.

He leans in. "You don't look eighteen."

"I'm young for my age, sir."

He grunts. "What's in your bag?"

"My clothes, sir."

"Open it up."

The girl loosens the drawstrings and holds the bag up. Blackborne reaches in, searches around with his hand and pulls out two books. He holds them to the binnacle light: *The Sea-Wolf* and *Sailing Technique*. "You've read these?"

"Yes, sir."

"Do you know where to throw the trash?"

"Over the lee side, sir."

"Show me."

The girl points at the dark sea. "There, the port side."

"You will serve as cabin boy until I can put you ashore. Crabbe, take him below to bunk in the saloon. Tell Cookie to show him his duties in the morning."

THE GIRL STANDS in the galley holding plates as Cookie loads them with fried potatoes and eggs. When the men come to the galley door, she hands them a plate and they go into the saloon to eat. Cookie wipes his pudgy hands on a towel and throws it on the counter. "I'm gonna relieve Sully at the helm. You get a plate ready for him when he comes." He puts on a jacket and a cap and waddles out of the galley.

A few minutes later the girl hands Sullivan a plate and starts to fill another plate for herself when someone shouts, "Bring some more coffee." The pot is on the stove, still percolating, the coffee black in the glass knob at the top of the pot. She takes the pot into the saloon and pours Blackborne a cup. The man called Crabbe turns his cup upside down and smiles at Marlin across the table.

"What did I say about doing that, Crabbe?"

Crabbe turns the cup right side up and then upside down again. "Does that double the bad luck?" Marlin glares at him and the girl falls against the table as the schooner lurches and the main boom swings slowly inboard and then slams out again as the wind catches the sail. Crabbe looks up at the skylight. "Sounds like Cookie is trying to gybe the main. You ever notice that Cookie is the only one who gets fat on his own cooking?"

"Shut up, Crabbe."

The girl carries empty plates back to the galley and begins washing up. She thinks about the crew. Sully is the big one with pale skin and reddish hair. Crabbe is the smaller and darker one with a long thin nose. And Marlin is the old one with a white beard. Blackborne comes in the galley and pours his coffee in the sink. "After you clean up here, go see Marlin. I want you to take the helm while the crew is eating."

"Yes, sir."

Blackborne climbs on deck, his broad back filling the companionway. He's bigger than Sully.

Cookie comes into the galley. "You ain't done washing up yet? What are you doing, waiting for Davy Jones to come for ya? Get this cleaned up so I can start dinner." Cookie goes to the saloon and heaves himself into his bunk.

The girl puts the last of the dishes away. Pig-eyes, that what Cookie has. She goes on deck and walks aft to Marlin at the helm. "Do you know how to box a compass?"

"No, sir."

"Don't sir me. I ain't no officer. Now come here and look." She steps next to him and looks at the compass card. "Start at north and name each point."

"North, North-North East—"

"Stop. It's North, North-by-East, North-North East, North-East-by-North, North-East, and so on. Start again." When the girl gets around the compass card without making a mistake, Marlin tells her to repeat it counterclockwise. "Now go stand by the foremast and practice until you can do it in both directions, then come back and show me." She goes forward and watches the bow of the schooner roll into the ocean swell. She doesn't need to practice. The compass is simple enough. She returns to Marlin and recites the points in both directions without making a mistake. "How many points are there?"

"Thirty-two."

"Show me four points off the starboard bow." The girl points with her outstretched arm, an imaginary line running just aft of the fore shrouds. "Good. Now take the helm. The course is South-East-by-South." The girl holds the wheel in both hands and looks at the compass. She over-steers at first, until she gets a feel for the schooner sliding through the sea, and then she takes control.

The sea is a dark green except where the waves crest and turn the water a dull white. Overhead a high fog absorbs the sunlight. The world is gray. No land or ship in sight.

"It looks like you got the feel of it." Marlin moves around to face her. "Where's the wind?"

"On the starboard quarter."

"Where do you feel it?"

"On the back of my neck. On the right side."

"Keep it there." His eyes smile. "I'm going below. If the wind changes and you can't hold the course, sing out. And keep an eye on the sails and the horizon. Remember, steer by the wind."

THE GIRL CARRIES the coffee pot and two cups aft, balancing herself on deck with her knees bent and her feet apart. The sun is below the horizon and the sea is turning dark. Crabbe is at the helm and Blackborne is standing beside him. The girl pours the coffee for them. Blackborne looks aloft and then back at the sea. "Head south one point."

"Can you put the compass light on? I can't see it."

"You don't need the compass. Where does the sun set?"

"There." Crabbe points at the fading light on the horizon.

"Well?" Blackborne sips his coffee and without making a face, flings it overboard. When Crabbe doesn't answer, Blackborne turns to the girl. "Where's south?"

The girl faces the fading light and stretches out her left arm and points.

"Why don't you need the compass."

"I am a compass."

As the sun rises above the land, the schooner drifts toward a wide bay. The girl stands on the foredeck breathing in the morning freshness. She expected to feel the wind and the sea, and under her feet, the wooded deck. But she didn't imagine the green sea turning deep blue or the grey sky becoming pale in the sun's brightness or the dark colors of the north changing to the light pastels of the south.

They anchor inside the breakwater and put the boat over the side. The girl helps clear the deck until Blackborne calls her aft. "Get your bag and be ready to go ashore." The girl holds her bag in one hand and follows Crabbe into the schooner's boat. She sits in the bow and Blackborne sits in the stern while Crabbe rows them ashore. When the bottom of the boat scrapes the sand, the girl jumps out and walks up to the line of debris at the high-water mark. The beach is wide and rises up to a town of low buildings, backed by brown hills that surround the bay. There is no one else on the beach. "Wait here." Blackborne walks toward the town carrying a tan briefcase stained with oil.

Once Blackborne is out of sight, Crabbe looks up and down the beach. To the north is a small building with dried palm leaves for an awning. "Let's go get a beer."

"I don't drink beer."

Crabbe looks disgusted. "Maybe you should start." He walks up the beach, leaving footprints in the sand, until he moves sideways into the shadows of the palm leaves. The late-morning sun turns harsh and the girl holds her hand to shade her eyes as she looks out at the bay. The schooner, her white topsides shining where the sun strikes them, rides motionless on the calm water, her masts and topmasts rising above the breakwater. There are no other boats in the harbor.

Blackborne returns and looks up and down the beach. "Can you row?"

"Yes, sir."

"Shove off and row me back to the schooner."

As the girl rows, she watches the bar with the palm-leaf awning. No one is there. They reach the schooner and the girl catches onto the rail, letting Blackborne climb aboard first. "I thought you were going to leave me here."

"I'm short-handed."

"Thank you, sir."

"What?"

"I want to stay on the schooner."

"Wait in the boat to rig the tackles." Blackborne walks aft. "Get the schooner underway, Marlin. We'll head farther down the coast."

They haul the boat aboard and the girl helps lash it on deck. Marlin shows her how to work the anchor winch and when the anchor is up and down, they hoist the mainsail. The girl tails off for Sullivan, and as the gaff sways aloft she senses a force hidden in the spread canvas. They go forward and raise the foresail and staysail, and with the sheets free, the booms swing from side to side in the light breeze. Blackborne hardens the mainsail sheet and the schooner gains way and breaks out the anchor. "Away aloft, boy. Report what you see."

Marlin grabs the girl's arm. He's short but powerful, his grip on her arm leaves red marks. "Go up the weather shrouds." She climbs up the ratlines and stands on the crosstrees. Beyond the breakwater the ocean spreads out to the horizon, and on the other side the town recedes into the barren hill. She looks ahead and calls down. "Rock, three points off the port bow." She climbs to the deck and stands next to Marlin. "Did the captain want to see if I was afraid of heights?"

"He wanted see how good your eyes are."

Blackborne calls the girl aft. "Get your kit and move forward to the fo'c'sle. You have the afternoon watch."

As the girl heads forward, Marlin smiles at her. "Welcome aboard the *Ellie*."

THE GIRL STEERS with the wind on the starboard quarter. The day is clear, with a few clouds low on the horizon. A pod of dolphins appears and swims with them, diving before the bow as if they were showing the schooner the way through the sea. At the end of her watch, Marlin comes aft. "You have a quiet watch?"

"Yes. Dolphins swam with us for a time."

"That's for luck."

Blackborne climbs out of the aft hatch and glances at the sails. "Did you finish high school?"

"Yes, sir."

"Marlin, take the helm and bring the schooner into the wind. He turns back to the girl. "Haul in the mainsheet." The schooner begins to dive into the waves and spray sweeps over the foredeck. "What makes the schooner sail into the wind?"

She looks at the curve in the mainsail. "The wind on the outside of the sail has to travel over the curve, so it moves faster than the wind on the inside. That gives the sail lift."

"That lift pushes the sail sideways, not forward." He waits. "What resists the sideways motion?"

She's puzzled. "The keel?" She looks at Blackborne and then back at the mainsail. "Yes, the keel. It drives the schooner forward."

"What happens when you point too high on the wind?" He nods to Marlin and Marlin heads the schooner closer to the wind.

"She stalls."

"What else?"

"She makes leeway."

"Marlin, put the schooner back on course." He nod to the girl. "Let out the sheet and read the log."

The girl squats at the taffrail and studies the dial on the face of log for a moment.

"Twenty-six."

"Twenty-six what?"

14

"Miles."

"Nautical miles. Come below and write up your watch." She follows Blackborne down the aft companionway. The chart room is to port, before entering the aft cabin, a small cubbyhole with the navigation table built against the forward bulkhead and no place to sit except for a bunk on the port side that extends aft into the lazaret. Blackborne switches on the light over the navigation table and picks up a book. The light catches the heavy ring on his left hand, a gold wedding band. "I want you to keep the ship's logbook." He opens the book to a new page and lays it on the table. "Write the date at the top of the page and draw five columns: Time, Log, Course, Weather, and Comments."

"What kind of comments?"

"Anything that happens during a watch, a course change, weather change, or sail change."

"What about sighting dolphins? Should I comment on that?"

For a moment Blackborne's dark blue eyes search her face. "Sighting land birds and seagrass is more significant." He picks up a laminated card. "This is the Beaufort scale with a description of each wind force. Memorize it." Blackborne leaves the chart room and the girl begins writing up her watch. When she is finished she flips the logbook to the first page: Schooner *Eleanor Mooreland*. She turns the page to the crew list:

Andrew Blackborne, Capt.
Marlin Verde, Bo'sun
George Abner, Cook
Michael Sullivan, Seaman
Geofrey Crabbe, Seaman

She draws a line through Crabbe's name and writes her name below:

Darryl Simmons, Seaman.

THE SCHOONER ROLLS easily in the morning calm as the sails hang in the air. The coast is to port but it's too far off to see land. Sullivan comes aft to relieve the watch and Darryl points at the sea. "Look."

Sullivan follows her outstretched arm. "It's a sea turtle. I'm gonna get one after my watch . . . There's another one." The sea turtles float on the surface, the tops of their shells drying in the sun. Sullivan takes the helm and Darryl goes below to the chart room. When she returns to the deck, Blackborne is standing next to the helm. "Bring the coffee pot and cups."

Darryl goes in the galley where Cookie is cleaning up breakfast. "Well, pretty boy, I didn't get much help out of you before Blacky sent you to the fo'c'sle."

"The captain wants some coffee." The pot is on the stove, slowly percolating, the coffee black.

"Well, get him some." She takes the pot and two cups and heads back to the helm. She hands out the cups and pours the coffee and watches as Blackborne takes a sip and then throws his coffee over the side. "Come with me. Bring the coffee pot." She follows Blackborne down into the galley. "Cookie, what did I tell you about keeping the coffee warm?" He throws his cup and hits Cookie on the chest. "Hand me that." Darryl gives him the coffee pot and Blackborne throws it and hits Cookie on the forehead and the black coffee runs down his face and collects on his belly. "Don't let it sit percolating on the stove. Take the filter out when it's done." Blackborne continues to stare at Cookie. "Well?"

Blood begins to seep from the cut on Cookie's forehead. "Yes."

"Say, 'yes, sir.'"

"Yes, sir."

GUNSHOTS. Darryl hops out of her bunk and up the forecastle ladder. Sullivan is standing near the main shrouds shooting at a sea turtle with a pistol. "Damn, can't hit a thing with the boat rolling like this." He opens the cylinder of the revolver, takes out the spent shells and reloads. Blackborne walks down the lee side of the deck, picks up an iron belaying pin at the mainmast and coming up behind Sullivan, taps him on the side of the head. Sullivan flinches and Blackborne grabs the revolver and jerks it out of his hand. "What did I tell you when you signed on? No alcohol, no drugs, and no guns."

"Aw." He feels the side of his head. "I was just trying to get a turtle."

"You leave the turtles alone. We share the sea with them." He unloads the revolver and throw the cartridges in the sea. "You'll get this back when you sign off." He looks down at the deck. "Get a bucket and wash down. You," meaning Darryl, "get a broom and sweep after him."

THE NIGHT SKY is overcast and the only light is the phosphorescent plankton, churned up by the bow-wave as the schooner slides through the sea. Darryl is alone on the middle watch and she enjoys the feel of the schooner under her control. She looks forward to make sure no one is on deck. Blackborne doesn't stand a watch but he is often on deck, especially at night. She takes the used rag from her pocket and throws it over the side.

Blackborne comes out of the aft cabin. "Go make a pot of coffee." She gives up the helm and goes forward and down into the galley. While she is walking back with the coffee pot, there's a thud and then scraping along the port side of the schooner. They have hit something. She looks over the side as a small boat wobbles into the schooner's wake. The boat is empty. "Back the staysail." Darryl puts the pot on the cabin top and runs forward as the schooner comes into the wind. They heave-to and Darryl looks to windward but it's too dark to see anything, even the horizon is lost in the night. "Put the boat over the side." Marlin appears and they lower the foresail and ready the boat. As Marlin rows, Darryl kneels in the bow, sweeping the sea with a flashlight. Nothing. She looks back at the schooner. The starboard light is a green point, just visible in the darkness. Marlin rows into the wind until he has to rest on his oars. Darryl listens and then calls out. Nothing. Marlin begins rowing again, now in a circle. They don't find anything, not even the boat they hit. Marlin turns around, letting the wind drive them back to the schooner.

"We wait for daylight."

When light appears in the east, Darryl is on the main crosstrees with the glasses. She sweeps the horizon to windward and then to leeward, all round the schooner. A pair of seabirds fly past, black and white terns, skimming the waves. Nothing else. She returns to the deck and walks aft to where Blackborne and Marlin are waiting. She shakes her head.

Marlin stares off at the horizon. "The sea is a cruel mistress."

"The damn fisherman should have carried a light."

MIDDLE WATCH. Darryl climbs up the midships companionway and surveys the night. The land breeze holds steady and the sea is calm with just wavelets slapping the side of the schooner. A light off the port bow flashes. Blackborne is near the helm, watching her approach. "Do you know any geometry?"

"Yes, sir." She likes geometry because it's about shapes and she can picture them in her mind. "I had two years in high school."

Blackborne pulls the brass cover off the compass. "Check the relative bearing to the flashing light and tell me when it's forty-five degrees off the bow."

Marlin remains at the helm as Darryl watches the angle of the flashing light open up. "Now." She looks up. "The light bears forty-five degrees off the bow."

"Read the log and call me when the light is abeam." The schooner glides through the night without effort, as if she had subdued the sea. The middle watch is long and she hopes she doesn't get sleepy. The ship's clock chimes four bells and a few minutes later she calls Blackborne. "The light is abeam."

Blackborne checks the bearing of the light. "Read the log." Darryl gives up the helm and stoops over the taffrail log. When she turns back to Blackborne, he is smiling at her. Why is he amused? "What's the distance to the light." She stares at him. "Think of the triangle." What triangle? Then she sees it, the geometry problem. The two bearings and the schooner's course form a right triangle, so the distance to the light is the same as distance the schooner has traveled. She looks at Blackborne. It's her turn to smile. "The distance to the light is four and a half miles."

"We heave-to when Sullivan comes on watch."

THE SUN RISES over the barren hills behind the town, and as the schooner enters the bay, the wind dies and they lower the sails. Blackborne gives Darryl the helm. "Take the schooner in near the yacht club and decide where to drop the anchor." The helm feels different under power, especially in calm water. She brings the schooner into the shadow of the hill that protects the harbor. "Allow for more room to swing at anchor." She turns the schooner in a half circle and puts the engine in neutral and Marlin lets go the anchor near the other yachts.

Blackborne goes below and returns to the deck with his briefcase and Sullivan rows him ashore. Sullivan returns while Marlin and Darryl are rigging the awnings. "We got a lot of work ahead of us. Wash down the deck, Sullivan. We'll oil it as soon as it's dry."

"Wash it down yourself. I'm done here." Sullivan goes down the forecastle hatch. He returns carrying his seabag on his shoulder and walks to where the boat is tied. "Row me ashore, boy."

Marlin steps between them. "No one's rowing anyone ashore. The captain don't like it if you run."

"Blacky ain't here and I ain't stayin'. This ain't some kind of prison ship." Sullivan walks to the other side of the schooner and hails a sloop anchored nearby. A man climbs in the cockpit and looks toward the schooner and Sullivan waves. "Can you give me a lift ashore?"

The man waves and climbs in his dinghy and rows to the schooner. "Hallo. Is something the matter?"

Marlin points at Sullivan. "He doesn't have permission to go ashore."

"What's that? Is he sick?"

Sullivan climbs in the dinghy. "No, I ain't sick. I'm just sick of this schooner. Give way." The man in the dinghy shrugs before shoving off.

Darryl and Marlin watch them until they reach the yacht-club landing. "We'll do without him." They begin cleaning the deck.

Blackborne hails the schooner and Darryl rows to the yacht club to pick him up. "Where's Sullivan?"

"He packed his seabag and left."

"Take my briefcase and put it in the aft cabin." He turns and walks back through the yacht club and Darryl rows back to the schooner.

Later in the day Marlin and Cookie go ashore to buy supplies and Darryl gets out the linseed oil and uses a rag to spread the oil on the deck. There is little wind in the harbor and it's hot even under the awnings. She puts the oil away and sits on the forward cabin top, waiting for the oil to dry. They will need another crew now. The captain is probably looking for someone. There are a dozen yachts in the harbor. Some are going north and some south. Maybe he'll find someone who wants to go west.

Marlin and Cookie return and Darryl helps carry the supplies below, mainly fresh food, potatoes, onions, carrots, eggs, a lot of egg and some beef and chicken. They will have to eat the meat soon. The schooner has no refrigeration.

Marlin comes in the galley where Cookie and Darryl are cleaning up after dinner. He hands Darryl a straw hat. "I bought a couple of these in town. You need one in the tropics." She puts the hat on and wants to look in the mirror but Marlin is watching her. "A good fit. Let's all go to the yacht club and take a shower."

"I don't need a shower."

"Cookie, you been needing a shower for over a month. What about you, boy?"

"You two go. I'll watch the schooner and go when you come back."

Marlin looks at her for a moment. "Right then."

When Marlin and Cookie return to the schooner, Darryl rows to the yacht club. She hesitates at the entrance of the showers and then goes in the women's side. She can always say she couldn't read the sign. The shower feels good and she lets the sun-warmed water run down her back. She puts on clean underclothes, boxer shorts and a tight, sleeveless t-shirt. Beneath a lose fitting plaid shirt, she wears a pair of broad suspenders to hold up her baggy trousers. In the mirror she is tall and thin with her hair combed straight back. It will need cutting soon. She steps closer to the mirror. She has dark hair and blue eyes, like Blackborne. Her nose is straight and her chin is strong. They are her disguise. If you expect to see a boy, then she's a boy.

In the evening the workers at the yacht club give a party and invite all the yachts in the harbor. Marlin and Darryl go and the yacht-club workers serve them turtle stew from a large iron pot. The stew is red with chunks of meat. "The captain says we share the sea with the turtles."

"He admires the sea creatures. They aren't as foolish as most people."

"He told you that?"

Marlin laughs. "Sometimes it's not hard to know what he thinks." Darryl takes a sip of her beer and looks down at Marlin's bare feet.

"Why do you have animals tattooed on your feet?"

"The pig and the rooster. They are for luck."

"Why a pig and a rooster? Why not some other animal?" She doesn't like the beer and hands the bottle to Marlin.

"Some sailors tattoo themselves with other animals. The shellback turtle is one. It's not for luck, though. It's for showing that they have crossed the line."

One of the yacht-club workers comes over and sits next to Marlin. "You like the festival?"

"The stew is good." Marlin raises his bottle of beer. "The beer is good, too." There's a pause, each waiting for the other to speak. "How do you catch the turtles?"

"Simple. When the sea is quiet, the turtles lie in the sun on top of the water. We row up and grab them. They have too much air to make them float and they can't get away fast."

The next afternoon, after overhauling the rigging, Marlin and Darryl sit near the helm. Marlin sips his coffee. "I thought you would be leaving us instead of Sullivan."

"I'm not leaving. The captain is going to teach me navigation."

"He told you that?"

"No, but he likes to teach."

"Yes, that's true." Marlin looks off at the palm trees that line the esplanade on the other side of the harbor. "He tried to teach me navigation but I didn't take to it."

Blackborne returns to the schooner and Marlin watches him. "And?"

"The police have him."

"I don't mean Sullivan."

26

"It isn't your problem, Marlin."

"I know, but I want to know where we're going."

"We're going southwest. Get the schooner ready to move over to the fuel dock."

At the fuel dock Darryl squats over the hose as she fills the schooner's water tank. Two policemen bring Sullivan down to the dock. He's too hung over to walk straight. The policemen heave him onto the deck, salute Blackborne and walk away. Sullivan lies on the deck, dirty, his clothes torn. Blackborne takes the water hose out of Darryl's hand and sprays Sullivan. He rolls over and sputters. "Hey"

"You have run from my schooner. Next time I'll leave you in jail and let them tattoo your face." He hands the hose back to Darryl. "We get underway as soon as the water tank is topped off."

SECOND DAY AT SEA. The sky is overcast and squalls sweep in from the northeast as the schooner labors in a heavy sea, pitching into waves that crest and break over the bow. Marlin lowers the jib and Darryl climbs out on the bowsprit to lash it down. When the bowsprit slams into a wave she holds on with both hands, turning her face away from the spray that shoot up over her head. She inches toward the jib stay and as she reaches up to grab the loose halyard, it whips her watch cap off and the cap tumbles in the wind and falls in the schooner's wake. Marlin shakes his head. "It's going to be a long passage."

They reef the mainsail and the schooner rides easier but the deck is still wet as spray flies over the weather bow. Blackborne calls Darryl aft. "Read the log." She bends down, holding on to the taffrail as the stern of the schooner falls on the back of a wave. They go down in the chart room. "Plot our dead reckoning position." He watches as Darryl draws the schooner's course from yesterday's dead reckoning position. "Use the left or right edge of the chart to measure distance."

She looks up from the chart. "Yes?"

"The top and bottom of the chart are inaccurate." He waits.

She looks back down at the chart and then pictures the earth as a globe with latitude and longitude lines on it. The distance between the latitude lines remains the same but the distance between the longitude lines changes. She looks up. "As the longitudes move to-ward the poles, the degrees between them remain the same but the distance decreases."

Three days later the wind shifts to the northeast and the sky clears. They shake out the reef in the mainsail and set the jib again and the schooner drives through the blue sea. Blackborne comes on deck with the sextant and a stopwatch. He sits on the cabin top and calls Darryl over. "Take the sextant." She grabs it by the handle and rests it in her lap as the schooner rolls with the ocean swell. "Before you put it to your eye, move the shades so you can see the sun without being blinded." Darryl lifts the sextant and looks through the telescope, searching for the sun. "Now release the clamp and bring the sun down to the horizon. When the lower limb is on the horizon, rock the sextant easily from side to side . . . Is it on the horizon?"

"Yes."

Blackborne stops the watch. "Now read the altitude."

Darryl looks at the scale on the arc and then the micrometer. "Twenty-nine degrees and 42.5 minutes."

"How does the sextant work?"

Darryl looks at the instrument in her hand. "It has two mirrors, here and here."

"Why?"

She looks at Blackborne, his dark blue eyes amused. Yes, this is how he likes to instruct. She lifts the sextant up to her eye again. "So you can see the sun and the horizon at the same time . . . and in the same place."

29

"Come with me." They go below to the chart room and Blackborne points to a notepad. "I wrote the time when I started the stopwatch. Add the stopwatch time to it. Now write the altitude of the sun." Blackborne walks Darryl through the calculations of a sun sight and she plots the line of position on the chart. "I want you to take the morning and noon sights. If the weather's bad in the morning, take an afternoon sight."

"Yes, sir."

"Put the sextant away." The sextant is in its box resting on the navigation table. Darryl closes the box and opens the bottom drawer under the table. Sullivan's revolver is there. She hesitates and then remembers the revolver isn't loaded. She places the sextant next to it and closes the drawer.

THE SEA IS CALM and the schooner rolls gently and the sails flap in the windless air. The doldrums. Squalls march across the horizon and sometimes a squall reaches the schooner, bringing wind and rain, and then the schooner races through the water before slowing again as the squall passes away.

Sullivan walks aft to relieve her. He's late again, five minutes, ten minutes and now fifteen minutes. "You're late Sullivan."

"So what. You're not going anywhere." His bruises are healed but his face is sullen and he still wears the torn shirt he had on when the police brought him back to the schooner. A badge of honor, won in the backstreets of a port town. Sullivan takes the helm and Darryl goes down to the chart room. When she is finished writing the log she goes to the galley for her breakfast.

Cookie hands her a plate and she stares at the pancakes. "These are burnt, Cookie."

Cookie draws on a cigarette. "Yeah, they got left in the pan too long." He flicks ash in the sink. "That's all there is, 'cus there ain't no more batter left."

Blackborne comes into the galley and looks at the burnt pancakes and then at Cookie. He steps around Darryl and grabs Cookie by his shirt front. "Come." He drags Cookie up the companionway and then forward to the mast and forces him to the deck. "Stay here." Cookie tries to get up and Blackborne puts his foot on his chest and pushes him back down. "I said, stay." Marlin and Darryl watch from the companionway. "He's drunk again. Sober him up." Marlin goes for the bucket and Blackborne turns to Darryl. "Go search for his bottle." She knows where to look. She opens the rice bin and digs through the rice until she finds the bottle of rum. When she returns to the deck,

Marlin is throwing buckets of seawater over Cookie while Blackborne watches. Darryl holds up the bottle. "Where was it?"

"In the rice bin."

"Yes. We haven't had any rice since leaving port. Throw it overboard."

For the rest of the day Cookie moans and groans but doesn't say anything or look anyone in the face. That night Darryl is sleeping in her bunk when something heavy hits her in the face and she wakes up in pain. "You little prick. Where's my bottle?" It's dark in the forecastle but she can smell him. Fried grease. She scrambles to the end of her bunk and climbs up the forecastle ladder. Cookie stumbles around in the dark. "I'm gonna get you. You wait. I'm gonna get you." Sullivan tells him to shut up and Cookie goes back into the saloon and it's quiet. Darryl sits huddled at the foremast to catch her breath and then she gets a bucket of saltwater and bathes her face, washing away tears.

In the morning Darryl sits at the helm reading the compass with one eye, her other eye swollen shut. After breakfast Blackborne comes aft and looks at her. "Cookie do that?"

"Yes, while I was asleep in my bunk."

Blackborne turns and goes to galley. From the helm Darryl can hear Cookie yelling. When Blackborne returns, he is rubbing the knuckles of his right hand. "Shift your bag to the chart room. You bunk there from now on."

THE TRADE WIND comes out of the southeast and the schooner rolls down the waves, dipping her lee rail in the water. Darryl estimates the speed between seven and eight knots. She checks the log. Eight knots. Sullivan relieves her at the end of her watch and she goes below to eat breakfast. Cookie is clearing the galley and Marlin is in the head with the door open, looking in the mirror as he cuts his hair. He has the same hair she has seen in pictures of a greek statues, loose curls that fall over the ears. He's snipping off some of the curls and the gray cuttings cover his shoulders. She takes her potatoes and eggs and sits in the saloon alone until Marlin comes in and puts his comb and scissors away. "Can you cut my hair, Marlin?"

"Sure. Come to me during the afternoon watch and I'll cut it while you steer."

In the afternoon Darryl sits on the steering-gear box and Marlin combs her dark hair to one side and then the other, cutting the ends. "Why was Cookie complaining yesterday about not playing Neptune?"

"We crossed the line yesterday and Cookie wanted to celebrate. The captain doesn't like it. It's just an excuse for Cookie to get drunk. When I first crossed the line, Neptune dumped a lot of water over my head and made me run around the deck on my hands and knees until my knees bled. If you ask me, playing Neptune is just a way to bully the youngsters on board." Marlin steps around to face her, combs her hair forward and snips a little. The sun catches his steel belt buckle and the reflection blinds her for a moment. "When are you gonna tell the captain that you're a girl?"

She doesn't want to answer. "He can find out for himself."

"What if he already has?"

"Do you think he cares?"

"I think he likes you as a boy." He combs her hair straight back. "Go look in the mirror."

Blackborne isn't in the aft cabin so she goes in and looks in the mirror above the vanity. Marlin cut her hair short on the sides and left it long on top. The yellow ring around her eye has faded. In another week it will be gone.

THE SCHOONER ROLLS to leeward, a motion the crew no longer takes notice of. The sky is clear except for the clouds on the horizon. Darryl comes on watch and Marlin holds up a bucket. "I picked up all these squid off the deck while it was still dark. Some of them flew so high they hit the mainsail." The squid are pale and flabby and she wonders what Marlin wants to do with them. "I'm going to fry them for breakfast." He takes the bucket and heads for the galley.

Cookie comes up the midships hatch, making a sour face. "I can't even stay in my galley with people frying smelly sea vermin."

"Marlin says the squid taste good."

"Yeah? They look like shark guts . . . Go try some and see if you like it. I'll take the helm."

She goes down to the galley and Marlin hands her a plate. He has cut the squid into rings and fried them in a batter. There's no fishy smell. Blackborne and Sullivan are in the saloon eating and Darryl sits at the table with them. Sullivan cleans his plate. "There any more, Marlin?"

"No, but I made some coffee." Marlin comes in the saloon with the coffee pot and cups and they all sit at the table talking, mostly about food they once ate and look forward to eating again.

Darryl returns to the deck and looks at the headsails and then at the sea as the wind blows the tops off the waves. Something on the horizon catches the sun, a flash of light and then it's gone. She goes forward and springs into the fore shrouds and climbs to the crosstrees. There's something there, off the port bow. Cookie calls her to come down and take the helm. "Wait." The schooner sails through the blue sea and then she looks again, squints, looks away and back again, squinting hard this time. She returns to the deck and calls Blackborne. "There's something ahead, one point off the port bow. I think it's a boat but I don't see a mast."

"Take the glasses aloft."

She climbs up the ratlines again with the glasses slung around her neck. It's a yacht listing to port, part of her red bottom exposed to the sun. She's dragging something, a sea anchor. Darryl tries to steady the glasses. No. She's dragging her mast. Darryl climbs to the deck and goes aft. "It's a yacht. She's lost her mast and she's dragging it from the bow."

"You and Marlin lower the foresail and get the boat ready to put over the side." Blackborne takes the helm and heads the schooner toward the wreck. They heave-to upwind and put the boat in the water. Blackborne uses the glasses to study the wreck.

Marlin looks from the wreck to Blackborne. "It's not *Ariel,* is it."

"No." He turns Darryl. "Take the boat and see if there's anyone on board. Bring the logbook back." She climbs in the boat and shoves off. The boat rises and falls on the waves and she rows carefully around to the stern of the wreck and ties the painter to a stanchion. As a wave rises the boat up, she hops aboard. "Ahoy!" No answer. She climbs in the cockpit and looks forward. A 34-foot sloop, her mast broken off a foot above the deck. The life raft is still lashed over the cabin. The port deck is in the water and Darryl uses her hands and feet to climb down the companionway. Trash sloshes in the water that floods the saloon, clothes, dishes, books. She wades forward, wishing she had shoes on. No one in the head or the forepeak. She turns back to the saloon. There's someone huddled in the corner of the lee bunk, a boy, his forehead resting on his knees. "Hello." The boy doesn't move. "What's your name." No answer. Darryl goes to the galley and fills a cup with water. She tastes it to see if it's fresh and then takes the boy's wrist and puts the cup in his hand. She waits until the boy takes a sip and then she moves to the navigation table and begins searching. The logbook is in the drawer beneath the table. *Holiday*. Odd name for an ocean yacht. She turns to crew list:

Ezra Poindexter
Linda Poindexter
Jody Poindexter

She finds the passports in the same drawer. The boy, Jody, is two months older than her. In the locker underneath the drawer, she finds a sextant. She picks it up and examines it, a new one. She thinks of taking it, but no, she's not here to scavenge. She turns to the starboard bunk, takes a pillow and pulls it out of its case. She opens the drawers under the bunks and stuffs clothes in the pillowcase. She looks around. What else? She puts the logbook in the pillowcase. A wave washes over the wreck and the sloop rolls farther to port. She goes back to the boy and takes his hand. "Jody, we can't stay here. Do you hear me? We have to go . . . Jody?" She gently tugs the boy's hand. The hand is thin and bony. "Come. We're going to look for your mother and father." The boy's head come up, showing a face with freckles spread across his nose and under his dull eyes. He slowly unfolds his thin body and Darryl leads him up the companionway. She holds the schooner's boat steady and the boy climbs in without any help but he keeps his head down and doesn't look around.

Darryl rows back to the schooner, pulling hard as waves slosh over the bow of the boat. She grabs the rail of the schooner and tries to hold the boat steady as the boy climbs aboard. Blackborne comes to the side. "Take him to the saloon."

"He's lost his parents and he's in shock. He shouldn't be around Cookie. There's room in the aft cabin."

Captain raises his eyebrows and then nods. "Put him in the port bunk."

Darryl leads the boy into the aft cabin and over to the port bunk. "Wait here and I'll go get some water and something to eat." In the galley she opens a tin and takes a handful crackers and then fills a cup of water. Cookie comes from the saloon. "What are you doin' in here?"

"We found someone on the wreck. I'm getting something for him to eat."

Cookie squints until his eyes seem to disappear. "Ask next time."

She returns to the aft cabin and as she passes the chart room, Blackborne is looking through *Holiday's* logbook. The boy is sitting on the bunk just as she left him. She hands him the cup of water and then the crackers. The boy holds them, the cup in one hand and the crackers in the other. He looks at them.

"Drink and try to eat." Blackborne calls her to help hoist the boat on board. She waits until the boy takes a sip and then she goes on deck.

At the end of the first watch Darryl goes into the chart room to write the log. She hears the boy cry out and Blackborne comes in the chart room. "See what he wants." She goes and sits on the edge of the bunk and takes the boy's hand and after a few minutes she slides down off the bunk and sits on the cabin floor, still holding his hand.

In the morning she brings the boy a bowl of oatmeal and a cup of coffee with sugar and milk. He eats and drinks and when he is finished he puts the empty dish and cup on the bunk and huddles again with his knees up and his arms wrapped around his legs. "How do you feel?" But the boy doesn't answer or look up.

She brings the dishes into the galley and Cookie points aft with his chin. "What's the matter with him? Why can't he come here and eat with the rest of us?"

"It's shock. He needs time . . . and rest. People shouldn't bother him."

"So you gonna play nursemaid? Feed him and pet him until he's better? Maybe he's a girly boy. You like that?"

She looks at Cookie's broken nose. "Cookie, you're a fool."

"Watch what you say." He picks up a carving knife and points it at her. "I don't like smart-asses."

"Not many people do." She walks out of the galley and up the midships companionway.

DARRYL STANDS OVER the navigation table working out the noon sight. She plots their position and then measures the distance to an island. A little more that thirty-eight miles. She goes on deck and looks forward. All she can see is a thick cloud bank. When she turns to take the helm from Marlin, he stands and points. "There. Land Ho!" Jagged peaks rise above the clouds that hug the island. The peaks are dark, too far away to have any color. Everyone comes on deck to look. "We should make the island sometime tomorrow."

"Have you been there before?"

"Yes, many years ago. I'm looking forward to seeing it again."

"I think we are all looking forward to being in port."

"Yes, it's like that. When you are at sea you look forward to being in port, and when you are in port you look forward to being at sea again. That's a sailor's life, always wanting a change." Darryl takes the helm and Marlin remains next to her as the clouds surrounding the island thicken and the peaks disappear. "How's the boy doing?"

"He still doesn't talk and loud noises make him jump. I think he just needs more time."

"I heard you singing in the aft cabin."

"Yes? He seems to like my singing, as long as the songs aren't sad."

"Just don't sing on watch. It brings bad luck."

During the middle watch Blackborne comes on deck. Darryl is at the helm and he tells her to get Marlin and heave-to. "We wait until morning."

As soon as it's light, Darryl takes the helm again and heads the schooner into the mouth of a long, narrow passage. As hills rise on both sides, the schooner loses the wind and begins to drift. They lower the sails and Blackborne starts the engine. "Ready the anchor." The passage sweeps to the right, revealing a land-locked bay. Marlin lets go the anchor and when Blackborne switches off the engine, the stillness is uncanny, no wind, no waves and land all about them. They put the boat over the side and Sullivan rows Blackborne ashore.

Darryl and Marlin rig the aft awning and then Darryl goes into the aft cabin. "Come, Jody, come look at the island." When he doesn't move, she takes his hand and gently pulls him off the bunk and leads him up the companionway to sit under the awning. A narrow beach of gray sand is surrounded by a green jungle, mainly coconut palms. Farther inland a few houses or huts are visible and as the land begins to rise, the jungle gives way to the grassland that dominates the lee side of the island. "Look at the jungle. The green is easy on the eyes." She turns from the jungle to the boy. His brown hair is long and fine. She runs her hands through it, trying to straighten it and then brushes it out of his face. He doesn't flinch under her touch but when Marlin comes aft, he gets up from the cabin top and goes below again.

Blackborne and Sullivan return with a boat full of fresh fruit, bananas, papayas, pomelos and six loaves of bread. "Stow the supplies and get the boat on board." He goes aft and starts the engine. As they power out of the bay, Darryl and Marlin unrig the awning.

The island falls astern and as it loses its green color, another island appears off the port bow. They sail into the night, leaving the islands behind. Darryl relieves Marlin at the helm. "Why didn't we stay at the island? We weren't there even one night." She sits on the steering-gear box and looks up at the mainsail. "Why is the captain in such a hurry? There's nothing ahead of us but a group of atolls."

"He's looking for his wife."

His wife, of course, the gold wedding band. "What happened? Where is she?"

"I think she stopped at the island."

"She did? How? There's nothing there."

"She ran off with someone, a friend of his, or what used to be a friend. They took the sloop, *Ariel*."

"We're chasing another boat?" Marlin starts forward. "What's he going to do when he finds them?"

He shrugs. "I don't know. We have to wait and see."

DARRYL LIES IN HER BUNK and feels the schooner beginning to heel more. They are changing course. She climbs out of the aft hatch. The wind is on the port beam and off the starboard bow is a low atoll, palm trees visible above the waves breaking on the reef. There are no houses or huts, but there's a wisp of smoke rising through the palms. They sail along the southern side of the atoll until they reach the western end where they heave-to and lower the boat over the side. "Sullivan, row the boy ashore. Try the pass. You should be able to get through. And Sullivan, if you meet someone, let the boy do the talking."

Darryl sits in the stern of the boat, watching the waves mount the reef. As they enter the pass the sun shines into the water, lighting up the colors of the coral, mostly browns with some deep purples. Fish scatter. Sullivan holds the oars out of the water and a wave lifts the boat and drives it into the lagoon. The middle of the lagoon is a darker blue but the edges, where the sun shines on the bottom of white sand, the water is light green. The wisp of smoke is at the far end of the atoll and Sullivan rows slowly up the lagoon, sweating in the midday sun.

A small man is waiting for them on the beach, fully dressed, khaki trousers, white long-sleeved shirt and even black street shoes, but no hat. Darryl and Sullivan are wearing straw hats to protect them from the tropical sun, and shorts, and no shoes. The man is holding a cloth bag and grinning. "About time you got here. I am getting tired of this place."

"We saw your smoke."

"So you stopped for me, not just to pick up some coconuts."

Sullivan climbs out of the boat. "I wouldn't mind picking some coconut. I like to drink coconut milk."

Darryl looks around. No boat. "How did you get here?"

"How did you get here?"

"You can see our schooner." She points to the west. "Where's your boat?"

"If I had a boat I wouldn't be here, would I?"

45

Darryl walks toward the smoke. Is the man hiding something? "Where are you going? You think it's time for some sightseeing?"

"I'm just looking around."

"There's nothing to look at here." The man walks to the boat and puts his bag in.

Darryl looks at the fire. There's a jug, probably water. Not a camp, not even a shelter. "How long have you been here?"

"Long enough to want to leave." He looks at Sullivan. "Let's go." The man starts to push the boat off the beach. Sullivan helps him and they both climb in, Sullivan at the oars and the man in the stern.

Darryl runs down to the beach and splashes through the water. "Hey, wait." She climbs over the man. "You're in my place."

The man grins. He grins all the time. "You're too young to tell me what to do. Go sit in the bow."

As Sullivan rows down the lagoon toward the pass, Darryl watches the man. "You were left on the atoll, weren't you?"

"A lot of things have happened. Most of them don't concern you."

"You're coming aboard our schooner. We want to know where you come from."

"Everybody wants to know something. I wanna know why they sent a skinny kid to pick me up." The man's eyes are dark and flat and their lack of expression clashes with his fixed grin.

When they come along side the schooner, Darryl passes the painter up to Marlin and they climb out and stand on deck where Blackborne is waiting for them.

"Take off your shoes."

The man holding the bag looks down at his shoes. "I don't have any other shoes."

"It's not about how many shoes you have."

The man hesitates. "Are you the skipper?" Blackborne doesn't answer and then the man slips his shoes off and leaves them on the deck.

"Show me your bag." The man holds up the bag and Blackborne grabs it and searches inside. He takes out a bottle of whiskey. "You'll get this back when you leave the schooner."

"Or when you leave the schooner." Still grinning.

Blackborne looks at the man, his pale hair, his dark eyes and his grin. "Do you have a passport?"

"You don't need a passport on a deserted island."

"Hand me your passport."

The man pats the pockets of his shirt. "Here it is." He holds up his passport. Blackborne flips through it. "Viktor Kovacs." He looks up. "How did you get on the atoll?"

"Some unpleasant people decided to leave me there."

"You were marooned. Why?"

"They were a pack of thieves." Kovacs grins. "Or pirates. They acted like pirates, drinking and fighting and that sort of thing. It was very unpleasant and when I mentioned it to them, they took offense."

Blackborne studies him for a minute. "Mr. Kovacs, I'm going to put you back on the atoll unless you give me a reason not to."

"Captain, that would be very unkind. I will probably die there a horrible death, first of thirst and then of hunger. Is that what you want? Is that what any man wants? To let another man suffer and die alone? And for what? Because I want to keep my past to myself? What man doesn't? What man doesn't have his secrets?"

Kovacs is going to be trouble and the captain knows it.

"Mr. Kovacs, I will put you ashore in the next port. Cookie will show you where to bunk. When you are on deck I don't want you aft of the mainmast." He hands the passport to Darryl. "Log him. Don't put him on the crew list."

They hoist the boat on board and put the schooner back on course. After clearing the deck Marlin joins Darryl at the helm. "What did you see when you brought that man off?" Darryl tells him that he didn't even bother to make a shelter. "It looks bad. Someone wanted to get rid of him and left him there. He sounds like a Jonah and now we have him." Marlin spits over the lee rail.

FIRST WATCH. As the sun drops below the horizon, Blackborne comes on deck and checks the wind and the sails. "Go fetch a cup of coffee."

Darryl gives up the helm and walks to the midships hatch where Kovacs is sitting on the top of the ladder. "You're blocking the companionway."

"Little boys shouldn't be rude. They should speak politely to their betters, otherwise they may get spanked."

"If you don't mind, I need to get down to the galley."

"I don't mind a bit. On the other hand, your needs don't interest me. Perhaps you should think of some other pursuit than going to the galley."

"You don't make any sense." Darryl goes forward and down the forecastle hatch.

Sullivan turns over in his bunk. "Keep the hatch closed for chrissakes." Darryl walks through the saloon where Marlin and Cookie are in their bunks. She pours a cup of coffee and looks up the midships companionway where Kovacs is still blocking the stairs. She goes back up the forecastle hatch, trying not to spill the coffee, walks aft and hands the coffee to Blackborne.

"What took you so long?"

"Kovacs is sitting in the midships hatch. He wouldn't let me by."

"Hold my coffee." He walks forward and with the flat of his foot knocks Kovacs off the ladder. Kovacs falls down against the galley doorframe and blood starts to seep from a cut on his forehead. Blackborne climbs down and waits for Kovacs to get up.

"I could've broken my neck falling like that."

"Get in your bunk and don't interfere with my crew."

"Or what? You gonna flog me for sitting on a step?" Kovacs touches the blood on his face. "I'm bleeding. Is that what you want?"

"I told you what I want."

THE ISLAND IS SHAPED like a cone, with its peak rising up to catch the clouds as they float past. A barrier reef surrounds the island and after they sail through the pass, they enter a wide lagoon with waves crashing on the reef to seaward and a row of buildings resting quietly on the land side, facing the reef. Yachts, moored stern-to along a stone quay, ride uneasy in the trade wind. Behind the yachts stretches Portville, a colonial town of wooden houses and shops, with a cluster of two-story administration buildings in the center. Farther back a dense jungle grows up the windward side of the island and disappears in the clouds.

Darryl heads the schooner past the row of yachts, outside of where their anchors rest on the bottom of the lagoon. At the end of the row she turns the schooner into the wind and Marlin lets go the anchor and the trade wind blows the schooner back to the quay. They rig the gangway over the stern and when Kovacs comes aft with his bag, Blackborne shoves him onto the quay.

"You said you would give me my bottle of whiskey back."

"It was lost overboard." He grabs Kovacs' upper arm.

"Wait. Are you one of those men who likes taking candy from children?"

"We're going to the port officials." He leads Kovacs across the road toward the administration buildings.

Once Blackborne is gone, Sullivan and Cookie appear on deck in their shore clothes. "Where do you two think you are going?"

"We're going ashore and having us a beer." Cookie pushes past Marlin and Sullivan follows him.

After they cross the gangway Sullivan turns back to Marlin. "Blacky won't find me this time."

"This is an island. Where are you gonna go?"

Blackborne returns in the late afternoon and as soon as he comes aboard, he starts the engine. It sounds ragged, as if it isn't firing on all cylinders. The sound brings Marlin and Darryl aft. "Take in the gangway and stern lines and weigh anchor. We're taking the schooner over to the boatyard to get her hauled out." Blackborne heads the schooner across the lagoon and slowly guides her into the waiting cradle. Once the schooner is made fast, the boatyard winch pulls the cradle out of the water. Yellowish-brown weed covers the schooner's bottom. Blackborne walks around the hull, checking for damage, followed by Marlin and Darryl. "Get her cleaned off and painted, two coats of antifouling." Blackborne goes into the boatyard building and returns with a mechanic and they climb aboard and go down into the engine room.

Darryl and Marlin scrub and hose the bottom of the schooner clean and while they wait for it to dry, Marlin walks into town to buy some food. He returns with two large containers of fried noodles and two bottles of beer. Blackborne comes out of the engine room and they sit in the shade of the schooner and eat their supper. Darryl brings some of the noodles to the boy and urges him to go on deck. "We're in a boatyard now. The sun is about to down and the lights in town will come on." The boy eats but doesn't talk or leave his bunk. Blackborne comes into the aft cabin and sits at vanity and starts writing.

Darryl and Marlin start applying a coat of antifouling, Darryl working on the scaffolding and Marlin working below on the ground. When the sun disappears behind the island, the lights in the boatyard come on and they work into the night.

In the morning Blackborne tells Darryl to take the schooner back to the quay as soon as the second coat is dry. "If you have any letters to send, I'm going to the post office."

"No, I don't have any."

"Isn't it about time you wrote home?"

"No, sir. My home is here."

He looks at her for a moment and then nods. He takes his briefcase and walks out of the boatyard.

The lagoon reflects the afternoon sun, making Darryl squint as she brings the schooner back to the quay. She goes in the aft cabin where the boy has been so long, sitting in the bunk, his freckles have begun to fade. She takes his hand. "Come on deck. It's cool under the awning." He slowly stands and his thin body sways a little, even though the schooner is steady. Darryl leads him up the companionway and they sit together on the cabin top and watch the traffic pass on the road, mainly motorbikes and scooters, now and then a small car. "Look at the colors people wear, all bright primaries, red, green, and yellow, and then some blues and even purples." The boy doesn't respond so she stops trying to make talk and they sit quietly and the boy loses his tenseness. The bikes and scooters make a racket but the wind blows the exhaust away, into the town. When a scooter backfires the boy jumps. "It's okay. It's just a scooter. Look at the jungle. It must be cool in the shade. Let's take a walk and have a look." The boy stands and goes below to his bunk.

In the evening Marlin stays on the schooner and Darryl goes into town. Marlin told her about a market but when she finds it, the market is already closed.

Bars and Chinese shops line the side streets that lead
off the main road. Some of them don't have doors
and she looks into one of the bars. The light is dim
and a narrow horseshoe bar covers most of the room
in front. In the back are tables where sailors sit with
local women. Someone pushes Darryl into the bar.
"You're off the schooner, aren't you? Come and have a
drink." She turns to leave but there are three of them
and they crowd her as they walk to a table in the
back. One of the men falls over a chair and the others laugh. "Sit. I'll get some beer." Local women join
them, young and pretty, just girls really, with brown
eyes and big smiles with white teeth, their long black
hair brushed away from their face. Some have flowers
above their ears. A girl climbs onto a man's lap and
puts her arm around his neck. "You like me? You buy
me a beer?"

Another girl sits down next to Darryl. "I am Elizabeth. What's your name?"

"I'm Darryl."

"You don't drink beer? You don't like it?"

"No, you can have mine."

Elizabeth drinks from the bottle and when she puts
it back on the table, she laughs. "You have pretty blue
eyes. You give me a baby with blue eyes? " Then she

puts her hand between Darryl's legs. "Ah, you have a little one." She laughs again. "A little one is okay."

Darryl pushes her chair back and stands up.

A man on the other side of the table looks up. "What's the matter? You gotta piss already?" Darryl walks out into the night and takes a deep breath. She likes the island but she didn't expect this part, the side alleys in a port town at night. She walks back to the schooner.

The next morning Blackborne goes in the aft cabin where Darryl is sitting with the boy. "Get his bag together."

Darryl gets off the bunk. "You can't leave him here in this town. He's not ready and this is not a good place."

Blackborne doesn't look at her. "Get his bag and get him on deck."

Darryl goes in the chart room and stuffs her few belongs in her bag and returns to the aft cabin.

"What's the meaning of this?"

"If you are sending the boy ashore, I go with him."

Before Blackborne can reply, someone on the quay hails the schooner and he climbs on deck. An official in a uniform waves him ashore. Darryl looks out the hatch. The official talks to Blackborne and then the two of them walk into the town, heading toward the administration building.

Marlin walks aft and stands next to the companionway. "That looks like trouble."

"Do you think its Sullivan and Cookie?"

"The captain told me they are somewhere on the other side of the island. They both like their liquor a little too much and they were with Kovacs."

Darryl and the boy are standing on deck, both with their bags, when Blackborne and the official return leading Sullivan, Cookie, and Kovacs. As soon as they are aboard, the official pulls the gangway ashore and Blackborne starts the engine. "Take in the stern lines and weigh anchor." Darryl takes in the lines and Marlin goes forward and starts the anchor winch. Blackborne looks at the three men. "I'll put you ashore in the next port. In the meantime I expect you to do your duty. Sullivan, go get some rest so you can take the first watch. Cookie, go start supper."

Kovacs grins. "You got some duty for me?"

"Go below and stay in the fo'c'sle."

THEY CLEAR THE PASS under power and as Marlin and Darryl set the sails, Blackborne heads the schooner to leeward of a neighboring island with jagged peaks. "We're sailing on Friday, Marlin. Isn't that bad luck?"

"No, that's just a superstition. You don't want to believe in things like that."

The jagged peaks are the color of slate in the tropical sun and the trade wind coming over the starboard quarter is weak, making the schooner roll heavily in the ocean swell. "Set the light weather sails." Marlin goes to the sail locker and takes out the flying jib and carries it to the foredeck where Kovacs is sitting at the top of the forecastle ladder. Darryl raises the jib and Marlin sheets it home and goes back to the sail locker for the fisherman staysail. Kovacs jerks his head towards Darryl. "Hey, boy, how far is it to the next island?"

"About a week. More if this wind doesn't pick up."

"I asked how far, not how long. But a week will do."

Marlin and Darryl raise the fisherman staysail and the canvas bellies out between the masts. When they raise the main topsail, the sheet fouls and Darryl goes aloft to clear it. The schooner picks up a knot, maybe less but she rolls less. Darryl starts coiling down on the foredeck, watching the island to windward. It's close enough to see the waves breaking on the barrier reef. Marlin comes forward and tells Kovacs to get below and stay in the forecastle.

"Or what? You like kicking people down ladders too?"

Marlin smiles. "I have permission to do so."

"Really? Permission? You run this boat like a Sunday school." He does a child's squeaky voice. "Can I please have permission, Mr. Blacky, to take a piss."

"I ain't waiting much longer." His smile gone.

Kovacs starts down the ladder. "You know, you can't keep a good man down, not for long."

SECOND DAY at sea. Sullivan comes aft to relieve Darryl. "You're early, Sully."

"Yeah, I wanted to ask you something." He sits and takes the helm. "Have you seen Blacky's gold?"

"What gold? What are you talking about?"

"He has some gold, maybe lots of it. When he came and got us out of jail back in Portville, he paid our fine with gold coins. He didn't want to but those island police made him do it. Kovacs says that if he pays in gold coins he must have lots of them. Do you know where he keeps them?"

"No, I don't know anything about gold coins."

"You've never seen him pay for anything?"

"No, I haven't. I wasn't there when he paid the boatyard in Portville." The schooner wanders off course. "What are you thinking about, Sully?"

"I ain't thinking about nothing, if that's what you mean." He glances at her and then back at the compass. "But gold is something to think about."

In the evening Darryl relieves Marlin. "Sully was asking me about gold coins. Does the captain carry a lot of gold?"

"He has some gold coins for emergencies but I've never seen him use them. How does Sully know about them?"

"He said the captain used some to get the three of them out of jail in Portville."

"That means Kovacs saw them. They've been talking nonstop since we left port, mostly in whispers when I'm around. Now I can guess what they are talking about."

"Don't you think we should tell the captain?"

"About what? They just talk. Sailors are great talkers. They're probably having a gabfest in the fo'c'sle now that I'm on watch."

"Wait a minute." Darryl starts forward. The forecastle hatch is closed but the washboard isn't in place. She recognizes Kovacs' voice, low and insistent but she can't make out what he is saying. The other two, Sullivan and Cookie, are silent. Kovacs' voice drones on and on, until Darryl begins to nod off.

THIRD DAY at sea. Darryl finds Blackborne in the chart room and tells him about her conversation with Sullivan.

"Sullivan is a simple man."

"But Kovacs isn't."

"What are you worried about?"

"They may be planning something." Blackborne doesn't react. "Greed can make men dangerous."

"You are talking about two cowards and a fool. I don't think I need to worry about them."

"Can't we isolate Kovacs? Lock him in the engine room or something?"

"And let him sabotage the engine? No, let it be." Blackborne leaves the chart room and Darryl sits down on her bunk. Why does she worry and they don't? The captain and Marlin run the schooner and think nothing can happen to them. But if there is any trouble, it will be trouble for her.

FOURTH DAY at sea. Darryl wakes from a heavy sleep. Someone is kicking the side of the steering-well above her bunk. She puts on her shorts and shirt and goes on deck. Cookie is at the helm. Darryl looks at the sea and sky and the horizon and then the sails. It's a habit now. "Where's Marlin?"

"He's frying squid again."

She goes forward to the galley and Marlin hands her a plate of fried squid. "I got a bucket full of them during the morning watch." She takes her plate into the saloon and sits at the table with the rest of the crew.

While they all wait for second helpings, Kovacs talks about what he is going to do when they get to the next port. "I'll find a woman who has her own hut and I'll live like a white god." Blackborne ignores him but Sullivan listens with his mouth open.

"Some of the women are real pretty."

Kovacs grins. "From what I've seen, you don't really care how they look."

Darryl finishes her breakfast and takes her coffee on deck. No one is at the helm, then Cookie comes out of the aft hatch. He looks at her with his sullen face. "What are you doing, Cookie?"

"I was getting a drink of water. The squid make me feel sick."

"I thought you didn't eat any of them."

"It's the smell. I can't take the smell." He starts forward, holding his belly, and Darryl takes the helm. Cookie walks past the midships hatch and then goes down into the forecastle. What's he up to? She looks up at the mainsail and then back at the forecastle

62

hatch. He probably took a bottle of rum out of the captain's locker.

The sun rises above the clouds on the horizon, turning the morning air bright and the sea a deep blue. Darryl hardens the jib sheet, balancing the sails, so that the schooner keeps her course. She's thinking about getting another cup of coffee when a gunshot comes from the saloon. Darryl jumps up. Damn, Cookie took Sullivan's revolver. And what? Sullivan must have extra bullets. The boy, Jody, pops his head out the aft hatch. "It's nothing, Jody. Go back to your bunk." She runs forward to the midships skylight. Marlin is bent over the table and Sullivan is tying his hands behind him. Kovacs voice. "Cookie wants to carve you up a bit but we're all sailors here and I told him that's not how it's done at sea, isn't that right, Blacky?" Darryl moves around to the starboard side of the skylight. Blackborne is sitting at the table holding his arm. There's blood on his shirt. Sullivan steps around the table and jerks Blackborne's wrists behind him and starts tying his hands. She moves to the aft side of the skylight while trying to control her breathing. This was planned. Kovacs planned it. Somehow he found out about Sullivan's gun and then he made Cookie get it for him. Why didn't she think of that?

Kovacs is standing in the doorway to the forecastle, holding the revolver and grinning. "In some ways I'm like you, Blacky. I believe in doing things the right way, according the traditions of the sea. When we put you in the boat, I'll make sure you have some straws so you and the old bo'sun here can decide which one will eat the other one. That's how it's done, isn't Blacky." Kovacs steps forward. "Get them on deck."

Darryl hurries back to the helm. Cookie comes out the midships hatch holding a carving knife, followed by Marlin and Sullivan. Sullivan looks at the sky. "Nice weather we're having." He turns to Marlin. "At least you won't be gettin' wet in the boat. That's something."

"You should let Kovacs do the talking."

Blackborne and then Kovacs come out the hatch. "You two get down on the deck." Darryl starts forward and Kovacs waves the pistol at her. "Stay at the wheel. I want you to heave-to." She brings the schooner into the wind and hardens the main-sheet. Sullivan goes forward and backs the staysail and lowers the jib. "Sullivan, you and Cookie get the boat in the water." They lower the foresail and hoist the boat out of its cradle and lower it over the lee side. "Okay, now dump these two in the boat. Don't be too gentle." Sullivan and Cookie lift Marlin up and when the boat rises on a wave, they drop him in. "Well, Blacky, you have any last words? What? You gonna be stubborn to the last? You know that's not how it's done. The least you can do is say, 'You will pay for this.' I expect to hear it. It's part of this . . . this ceremony." He waves the pistol at Sullivan. "Throw him in the boat." Blackborne is too heavy for Sullivan and Cookie and Kovacs has to help them. When they drop him in the boat, Darryl starts forward again and Kovacs waves her back. "I told you to stay at the wheel."

"I want to go in the boat."

"You aren't going anywhere. I want you to stay here." He waves the pistol at Cookie and Sullivan. "These two can't navigate. That reminds me, where is that other boy. Let me see if I have any use for him." Jody jumps out of the aft hatch, and without looking at the men standing near the mainmast, he climbs on the taffrail and leaps in the sea. Kovacs grins. "I guess he's afraid of getting buggered." He looks over the side. "Let the boat go."

Darryl steps forward. "Aren't you going to leave them some water? They won't last more than a couple of days without it."

"A couple of days sounds about right." Kovacs walks aft and pushes Darryl. "You come with me." She follows him into the chart room and Kovacs bends over the chart. "Set a course for here." He points to an island. "What are you doing?"

"I'm calculating our position." She takes the parallel rulers and draws a line to the island. "We'll be sailing into the wind."

"So what. This is a sailboat. Now get on deck and make sure you steer that course."

She takes the helm. The boat is already drifting to leeward and the boy is untying Blackborne and Marlin. Something breaks in the aft cabin. The liquor cabinet. Kovacs comes on deck with two bottles of rum, the pistol now in his waistband. "Sullivan, let go that sail up there and come down to the saloon. It's time for a little celebration." Sullivan releases the staysail and Darryl brings the schooner into the wind. Sullivan and Cookie follow Kovacs below. They don't bother to set the jib or the foresail.

Darryl hardens the main-sheet and then goes forward and hardens the staysail sheet. The schooner heads high into the wind, to just before the sails shiver. On this point of sail the schooner rises and falls in the waves but makes more leeway than anything else. After two hours, she puts the schooner on the other tack. She doesn't know how long she can do this, keeping the schooner from making any real headway. In the afternoon she lashes the helm and goes forward to listen at the skylight. The three of them are drinking and laughing. Kovacs is doing most of the talking. ". . . just pathetic." He holds up a bottle. "The rum is out." Kovacs stands, holding on to the table. "You two stay here." Darryl heads back to the helm. Kovacs is drunk but it shows only when the schooner catches him off balance. He goes into the aft cabin and she can hear him searching for something. When he climbs back out he has a bottle in his shirt and teak box with brass fittings in his hands.

"What's in the box?"

"You keep your nose on the compass." He staggers forward, holding the box with both hands. It must be heavy. She can knock him over the side now but as soon as she thinks of it, he is at the main shrouds and it's too late. Darryl waits and then goes forward and looks in the skylight. Kovacs pries open the teak box with a knife and lifts the lid. Sullivan and Cookie stand to look. "What did I tell you. Gold." Kovacs tips the box over and gold coins spread across the table.

"It's a fortune in gold coins."

"Sully, you're a fool." Kovacs holds a coin up. "They're twenty-dollar pieces, about one-hundred of them. That's two thousand dollars."

In the evening Cookie comes on deck and walks aft. "If you're hungry, there's some potatoes on the stove." He goes down into the aft cabin. Darryl waits until he returns, carrying two bottles of rum, and then she follows him forward. In the galley she cracks two eggs in the pan with the potatoes and as she fries them she can hear the men in the saloon playing with the coins. She takes her plate and eats at the helm. When she is sure no one is going to relieve her, she goes to the galley again and makes a pot of coffee, adding a little sugar and canned milk. The men in the saloon are quiet and when Darryl looks in, they are swaying to the pitching of the schooner while staring at the gold coins on the table.

Every two hours, when the ship's clock chimes, she puts the schooner on the other tack. Just after midnight there's some shouting in the saloon and Darryl creeps forward to the skylight. Cookie is red in the face. "You ain't got no call to call me names. I cooked dinner. That's my duty. If you want to eat again, wait for breakfast. Duty is duty."

"Cookie, I tell you what your duty is and when I tell you to cook, you get off your fat butt and cook."

"You ain't no captain. You ain't even a real sailor."

"Shut your yapper."

Cookie takes up his carving knife and waves it in Kovacs' face. "See this? You don't tell me what to do."

"You're right. I don't tell you anymore." Kovacs pulls the revolver out of his waist band and shoots Cookie in the chest.

Sullivan jumps up. "Christ almighty, what are you doing?"

"Don't you want his share of the gold?

"What?"

"Get the blanket off his bunk and wrap him up so he doesn't bleed all over the cabin."

Darryl scurries back to the helm. Kovacs and Sullivan are little more than shadows as they carry Cookie's body out the midships hatch. They drop the body on deck and roll it to the lee rail. The bigger shadow, Sullivan, stands over the body. "He was a shipmate. We should say something."

"You're right." Kovacs clears his throat. "We commit this lousy cook to the sea."

When Sullivan doesn't move, Kovacs shouts at him. "Do it."

DARRYL STEERS THE SCHOONER through the night. An hour after sun rises she goes to the main skylight and looks in. Kovacs is sleeping with his head in his arms on the table and Sullivan is lying on the settee across from him, snoring softly. Darryl gets an iron belaying pin from the mainmast rail and goes down the midships hatch. The gold coins are stacked in two piles on the saloon table and the empty rum bottles are laid out in a row on the port bunk. Should she hit them on the head with the belaying pin? They are so drunk she probably doesn't have to. She nudges Kovacs. He doesn't move. She climbs on the settee to get around him and goes into the forecastle, takes the rigging knife out of the bo'sun bag and cuts two lengths of half-inch rope. She starts with Kovacs, pulling his arms behind him and tying them together. He wakes up, groggy, and tries to free his hands, and then Darryl remembers the pistol. She reaches around and grabs it from his waist. When Kovacs sees her with the pistol, he flops on the settee, inches forward on his back, and kicks her hand. She steps away, pulling the rope around his wrists tight. "What are you doing? I told you to stay at the wheel. Who is steering? Somebody has to be steering." He tries to kick her again and she shoots him in the leg.

Kovacs starts yelling and Sullivan sits up. Darryl ignores Kovacs. "Lie face down, Sullivan, with you hands behind you."

"What?"

She moves around the table and hits him in forehead with the butt of the pistol. "Now!" She kneels on Sullivan's back and ties his hands. "Get on the cabin floor and lean against the table stanchion." She ties his hands to the stanchion.

"I'm bleeding. Come and stop the bleeding. I don't have a lot of blood." She moves back to Kovacs and pushes him onto the cabin floor. He lands on his side and she ties him to the other table stanchion, then slits his trouser leg open and looks at the wound. Blood is seeping out of his thigh. So she missed the artery. She goes to the aft cabin and gets the first aid kit and wraps his leg with bandages.

Darryl washes her hands in the head, soaping them twice and drying each finger, one after the other. She ignores their complaining, shuts it out completely, to concentrate on what she has to do. She goes aft to the chart room. It's been twenty-four hours since Kovacs put the captain and Marlin in the boat. For most of that time she has held the schooner close to the wind. The log is inaccurate, so she estimates the schooner has made about fifty miles. She plots her position and then goes on deck and lets out the main-sheet until the sail is up against the shrouds, then she rigs a preventer on the main bloom. She heads the schooner down wind. It's an inefficient point of sail, plus the following sea rolls the schooner from rail to rail. For the first time she feels alone. She holds the wheel tight to keep the schooner from broaching and to keep her hands from shaking. She's tired but she can't sleep now. She has to find them.

It's time to take a sun sight but she can't leave the helm while running down wind, so she hauls in the main-sheet and heaves-to. After plotting her position she goes in the galley and cooks some oatmeal. It's quiet in the saloon and the table is bare now. The schooner has rolled everything off, the bottles, the glasses, and all the gold coins. Some of the coins have fallen on Kovacs and Sullivan. She checks their ropes. They are both sleeping

It's too early yet but she climbs into the shrouds anyway. The sky is clear and the sun shines bright on the sea. In conditions like these she can see ten miles from the masthead, but she will have to be closer, much closer, before she can spot a small boat on the open sea.

She climbs down and releases the staysail and turns the schooner down wind again. At noon she take a sun sight and plots her position. Thirty miles southeast of yesterday's mutiny. It's a race now. She hopes to reach yesterday's position before sundown. But how far has the boat drifted?

She puts the schooner back on course and takes the helm. The afternoon is clear but her mind is becoming foggy. Her head droops and her eyes slowly close while she clutches the wheel with both hands. Her head snaps up as soon as the schooner goes off course. This won't do. She heaves-to, letting the schooner drift down wind, and climbs in her bunk. She sleeps until evening and wakes dreaming of someone shouting from far off. She gets up and goes in the saloon and tells Kovacs to shut up. "Or I'll knock you on the head."

Sullivan complains. "Water. Give me some water."

"You'll get water when I find Captain Blackborne."

"What? What if you don't find him?"

"The kid's smart. He'll find him, won't you kid?"

"I told you to shut up, Kovacs."

"But you need help. You can't sail this boat by yourself. At least untie Sullivan so he can help you. We won't cause you any trouble. You can be sure of that."

She doesn't want to talk to them so she lets Kovacs have the last word and goes on deck and puts the schooner back on course.

She steers through the evening and into the night until she reaches the position of the mutiny and then heaves-to again. She rigs the riding light, just in case the boat is close enough to see the schooner. She goes in the galley and eats two fried eggs and drinks a cup of water, ignoring the two in the saloon. The captain and Marlin and Jody are without water and it hasn't rained. She has a day and a half, maybe two days at the most. What if she doesn't fined them? What is she going to do with those two in the saloon? She goes in the chart room and writes a description of the mutiny in the logbook, putting in every detail she can remember. The logbook is an official document. If she gets to port, it will support her story against whatever Kovacs says. Thinking about it makes her sick. She goes to the lee rail and the eggs come shooting out of her mouth and fall into the sea.

She wakes several times during the night and goes on deck to stare at the darkness. Just before dawn Kovacs and Marlin start yelling. In the saloon she squats down to look at them under the table.

Sullivan lifts head. "You can have all my gold, just untie me a little."

"You're shaking, kid. It's time you got some help."

She looks at Kovacs. "I'm tired, that's all."

"You're smart. You know what the law says? The law says that prisoners, especially wounded prisoners, have rights. You have to let the Red Cross visit me. It's a matter of your own humanity. You should think about that. About the law and about . . ."

"Kovacs, as far as you are concerned, I am the law."

She gives them some water to keep them quiet
and checks their ropes. Still tied good and tight.

As SOON AS THE SUN is up Darryl climbs to the
masthead and searches downwind. Maybe she drifted
passed them in the night. Maybe her calculations are
off. She searches upwind. The tops of the waves break
and white foam slides down their face. White, the
color of the boat. She could look right at it and not
see it.

She takes a sun sight and calculates how much
she has drifted in the night, then she estimates how
much the boat has drifted. She sails down wind until
noon and takes another sun sight. She knows where
she is, but where is the boat? She climbs to the masthead again and searches the horizon. Nothing, not
a cloud or a squall, nothing at all. When she starts
climbing down something catches her eye. There's a
flash of light off the port bow. The boat. They can see
the schooner and they are signaling. Probably with
Marlin's belt buckle. She jumps back on deck and runs
to the compass and takes a bearing and then heads
the schooner toward the boat. When she is close, she
heaves-to and lets the schooner drift down to them.
She can't stop waving.

Marlin rows up to the schooner and Blackborne swings aboard with one arm, his other arm tied to his chest with a strip of canvas. "Where are they?"

"In the saloon. Tied up."

"And the pistol?"

She lifts her shirt to show him the pistol.

Blackborne nods. He turns to the two in the boat. "Wait there." He goes down the companionway. Sullivan starts shouting as Blackborne drags him by his shirt and throws him on deck. Sullivan's bloodshot eyes are wide open, as he twists and squirms. "What are you gonna do?" He looks around and sees Darryl. "What happened?" Blackborne drags him over to the windward rail and Sullivan stares at the water. "You can't do this."

"Sullivan, mutiny is a capital crime." Blackborne shoves him over the side and Sullivan falls into the sea. "Get some water." Darryl hurries to the galley and returns with a pitcher of water and holds it up to Blackborne. "The others first." Blackborne goes below again and drags Kovacs on deck, shouting and kicking with his good leg. "What are you doing? I'm a wounded prisoner."

Blackboure looks at Darryl. "Did you shoot him?"

"Yes, in the leg."

Blackborne pulls Kovacs over to the rail. "Wait. Don't you know, I have rights. I demand a jury of my peers."

"There's no such thing." He shoves Kovacs over the side. "Where's Cookie?"

"Kovacs shot him and they threw him overboard."

Blackborne nods. "Bring some more water." She takes the empty pitcher to the galley and fills it again. Blackborne drinks until the pitcher is empty.

Marlin climbs aboard and walks to where Kovacs went over the side. "So they took up Jonah and cast him into the sea."

"Marlin, you will have to do the cooking for now."

Jody climbs out of the boat, his freckles prominent across his sunburnt face. "I can cook." He heads down the companionway and they hear him rummaging in the galley.

Marlin similes. "That kid talked the whole time we were in the boat. It was no use telling him to be quiet."

"Mr. Simmons, I'm promoting you to mate. Hoist the boat on board and get the schooner underway. The course is North-by-Northwest.

Mate

THREE DAYS OF CALM with the sun beating down on
the schooner. Darryl hauls up a bucket of sea water and throws it on the deck and the water spreads
across the hot wood and runs out the scuppers. The
water cools the wood for a few moments before it
evaporates in the still air. The sails hang limp and
lifeless, and without steerageway the schooner swings
leisurely around the compass, pointing at the cloud-
less horizon. There are no birds and the sea is empty
and smooth except for a swell, almost imperceptible,
coming out of the east.

The next morning the swell has taken on more
form, becoming higher and rounder, making the
schooner roll from side to side in the windless air.
Blackborne comes out of the aft cabin. "Mr. Simmons,
the glass is falling."

Darryl looks to the east where a dark cloud has appeared on the horizon. "A storm is coming."

"A tropical cyclone."

They've had some bad weather before, squalls and even gales, but this is different. They have to avoid the storm, at least the worst part of it.

"As soon as there's steerage, set the course." Blackborne continues to look at her, amused but not smiling. This is one of his lessons. Darryl has no experience to rely on this time, only some reading. What did her books say about hurricanes in the southern hemisphere? The storm is coming from the east. She turns her back to the dark cloud. It's rotating clockwise, so the low pressure is to the right. "We run to the southwest. We carry our sails as long as we can to run from the center of the storm." Blackborne nods and Darryl turns to Marlin. "Prepare the schooner for storm weather."

Darryl goes to the galley skylight and calls down. "Jody, cook up a big dinner and then make a soup for later." She gets out the washboards and inserts them in the hatches and then helps Marlin rig lifelines. They prepare a drag by tying the mooring lines together and fasten one end to the samson post on the stern and the other end to the three tires they use as fenders. They leave the drag coiled behind the main-sheet, ready to throw overboard.

The swell and the black cloud continue to grow, the cloud reaching into the sky toward the sun and the swell making the schooner rise and fall, as the sails slap against the rigging. "Marlin, double the lashings on the boat." The light dims as the cloud reaches the morning sun. "Captain, do we send down the top-masts?"

"No, we carry the topsails as long as we can."

Darryl and Marlin get the fisherman staysail out of the locker in the midships companionway and ready it to hoist. They both look up at the same time. A whisper of wind. "Mr. Simmons, we have steerage. Go aloft and shake out the topsail." Darryl jumps into the rigging. "Marlin, set the flying jib and then the fisher-man staysail." The whisper becomes a light breeze, filling the sails. Blackborne heads the schooner south-west, taking the wind on the starboard quarter. Darryl climbs down and springs to the deck. "You and Mar-lin go eat, then take the helm."

When Darryl returns to the deck the wind has increased and the schooner is making five knots, cut-ting through the smooth sea. As she walks aft the tops of the waves start to break and the sea begins to turn gray. "Do you think we can out run the storm?"

"No." He looks at the cloud devouring the sky. "The storm should edge north. Maybe we'll avoid the worst of it. Keep the wind on the quarter." Blackborne goes below. The wind continues to increase and the day grows darker.

Blackborne returns to the deck and stands next to Marlin at the mainmast. They watch the coming storm without talking. Marlin's worried but Blackborne isn't. Darryl grips the wheel with both hands. A gust hits the schooner and she looks up at the light-weather sails. The canvas is stretched tight under the strain of the wind aloft. They won't be able to carry them much longer,

THE BLACK CLOUD covers the sky and the day turns dark long before the sun is down. The schooner races through the sea with her lee rail constantly in the water. The rigging is taunt and for the first time Darryl hears it sing, a high pitched whistling, uncanny in the darkness of the day. The sun goes down and the schooner rushes into the night.

The wind whips up the sea and as the schooner dives down the face of a wave, the bow plunges into the trough and water washes over the deck. "Mr. Simmons, clew up the topsail and send it down. Marlin, down the flying jib." Marlin is already scrambling forward. As Blackborne reaches over to release the fisherman-staysail sheet, a wave breaks over the stern and throws him against the side of the cabin. The fisherman staysail bursts, as if it were a child's balloon, and the shreds disappears in the darkness. Blackborne pulls himself back to the wheel before the schooner can turn into the wind. Darryl climbs down to the deck and hauls in the topsail as it flies out to leeward and falls into the sea before she can haul it in. She meets Marlin at the sail locker stowing the flying jib. "The main now." Marlin lets go the peak halyard, scandalizing the sail but the wind drives the canvas against the rigging. Blackborne heads the schooner more to windward and they claw the sail down and drop the boom into the gallows. A wave crashes over the stern and washes Darryl down the deck to the foremast. She is on her knees trying to stand when Marlin lifts her up to her feet. They lower the foresail and then the staysail. The schooner continues to rush through the sea with only the jib set. Jody comes out the hatch with a pot of coffee when a wave boards the schooner at midships, knocking him down and washing him into the lifelines. He comes up without the coffee pot, holding on to the end of a halyard trailing over the side. Blackborne shouts something. Darryl doesn't know what. The wind and the sea are too loud to hear anyone talk or even shout. She heads aft and water whips off the top of the waves, stinging her face. Blackborne grabs her arm and talks into her ear. "Take the helm." Blackborne steps aft and throws the drag over the stern. The mooring line pays out and the tires on the end of the line tumble over the waves. When the line is all the way out, the tires catch in the water for a moment and then spring into the air as the schooner staggers down the face of a wave.

The jib sheet parts and Blackborne and Marlin grope their way forward to take in the sail. The schooner is now running downwind under bare poles, dragging three tires, and still making five knots. A wave breaks over the stern, slamming Darryl against the wheel as water washes over her. When she can see again, Marlin is standing on the cabin top, clinging to the mainmast but she can't find Blackborne until the water runs off the deck. He's caught in the fore shrouds, holding on to the turnbuckles with both hands. He gets up and steadies himself before making his way aft.

The schooner climbs the backside of another wave, rolls to port at the top and pauses before plunging down the face, burying her bow in white foam. She wallows in the trough, until the next wave crashes over her and sweeps the deck from end to end. Darryl holds her breath until the water pours off the deck and the schooner rise out of the sea. She wipes her face and concentrates on steering, trying to keep the stern to the waves that tumble toward them.

Blackborne stands in the steering well next to Darryl, his shoulders hunched as the schooner climbs a wave and then slides down into the trough. Darryl waits, holding her breath without realizing it, and then the bow lifts and the schooner rises over the wave. Two more heavy waves hit the stern and the schooner rides over them. Marlin is speaking but the wind snatches his words away. Blackborne grabs Marlin's arm and talks into his ear and Marlin starts forward. Blackborne bends down and puts his hand on Darryl's shoulder. "Follow Marlin." He takes the wheel and Darryl stands and looks aft at the sea. A wave tumbles toward the schooner and slams into the stern. Spray shoots up and the wind whips it into her face but the wave doesn't come aboard.

Darryl starts down the companionway and once she is out of the wind, she feels cold and wet. Her hands are stiff and her arms ache from holding the wheel against the pressure of the sea. Jody is in the galley serving Marlin. When Darryl enters Marlin looks up at the skylight. "Here comes another one." Darryl falls against the galley door as Jody drops the soup ladle, grabs the counter with one hand and steadies the stove with the other. The schooner rolls to port as a wave crashes into her. Somehow Marlin manages to keep the soup in his bowl.

"That bread smells real good." Jody hands Darryl a bowl of soup and a thick slice of bread. "You baked it in a hurricane?'

"I had to do something while trying to keep the soup and coffee from flying off the stove." Jody is wet too. The galley is wet, everything is wet. "Go eat in the saloon. You're just in the way here."

Darryl sits at the saloon table with Marlin and for the first time she realizes that hours have passed since the storm hit them. Marlin looks up at the water dripping from the ceiling. "The next chance I get I'll make a cover for that skylight."

THE THIRD DAY after the storm Darryl climbs to the crosstrees and looks to the west. Somewhere ahead is land, a pair of atolls. The morning sun is still low and in the west the sky fades into the sea. As the sun climbs higher and the horizon clears, the black outline of Nott Atoll appears and then the white surf breaking on the windward side becomes visible. The atoll is a horseshoe-shaped with just a few coconut palms on a narrow stretch of bleached coral. The schooner passes to the south, close enough to see the broken reef on the leeward side. The atoll is small and uninhabited.

From the crosstrees Darryl can see Manulele Atoll just a few miles ahead. It's a round atoll with a barrier reef and a large island in the lagoon. As they approach the atoll, a low ridge running down the middle of the island slowly turns from black to green. Marlin heads the schooner along the southern side of the reef where low islets, bare and white, reflect the morning sun.

Darryl climbs down to the deck and walks aft. "There's something on the reef to the north. It looks like a wreck." She takes the helm as Marlin goes forward to ready the anchor. The schooner sails through the pass and turns up the lagoon with the wind astern and the mainsail sheeted out. The bottom of the lagoon is white sand spotted with dark shadows that mark clumps of corral. The schooner sails parallel to the beach and when she is in the lee of the island, Darryl turns into the wind and Marlin drops the anchor. The lagoon is still, except for the waves breaking on the reef.

THE WRECK ON THE REEF is recent. It lies with its bottom, still red, facing the lagoon and its deck facing the sea. It was a schooner, its two masts now rolling in the surf that washes across the reef. A man carrying a rope appears and walks along the topsides of the wreck. He doesn't have a shirt on. An Islander. He drops behind the hull and disappears.

Darryl turns toward the island. A white beach and then a line of palms that dwindle to pandanus trees to the south. Outriggers rest under the palms, partly protected with dried fronds. With so many outriggers, there must be a village on the island but nothing is visible from the schooner, except a tin roof with a cross rising above the palms. Farther back, the jungle spreads out in the distance and runs up the low ridge that divides the island.

Two Islanders drag an outrigger to the water and paddle a white man out to the schooner. As they come alongside the white man, in clothes that were once white, grabs onto the rail. "Can I come aboard?" He climbs aboard without waiting for a reply. "You've come just in time. I need to get a load of copra off to Newtown in Hawaiki." The man has a sunburnt face and blurry gin eyes under a dirty panama hat. "My name's Higgens, I'm the local trader here. A hurricane came through here a few days ago and the *Tantra* dragged her anchor. Now she is just a wreck." He points to the wreck lying on the reef. "We managed to get all the copra off and now it is drying in the sun. It will be ready in a couple of days and then we can load it on your schooner."

"This isn't a copra schooner."

Higgens looks around the deck. "There's plenty of room here." He looks back at Blackborne. "You'll have to go to Newtown anyway to report the loss of the *Tantra* and the death of Captain Blix and his mate."

"Mr. Simmons, put the boat over the side." He turns back to Higgens. "You, get in your outrigger."

Higgens hesitates and then climbs in his outrigger and pushes off. "We'll talk tomorrow after you've had time to rest up." The Islanders paddle to the beach and drag the outrigger back under the palms.

"Mr. Simmons, row me ashore."

As Darryl pulls the boat up on the sand, the Islander who was out on the wreck lands his outrigger farther down the beach. He stands next to it, wearing a blue and white lavalava and his bare chest reveals an intricate tattoo of thin swirls covering his right shoulder. There is no one else on the beach. Darryl stays at the boat and as Blackborne walks inland, a young woman steps out of the shadows of the palms and the Islander leaves his outrigger and walks quickly to her side. The woman steps toward Blackborne.

"I am Masina. This is my cousin, Rangi. Come, you are welcome here." Masina is an island beauty, with golden skin, dark eyes and dark, wavy hair falling down her back. Her red and white lavalava is wrapped tight under her arms, leaving her knees bare. Rangi is Masina's male counterpart, powerful and handsome, except for his expression, which is haughty, as if he has no use for white people.

Blackborne smiles, lowering his head. "I am Andrew."

"You are the captain of the schooner? Captain Andrew. Come, we prepare a feast for you." She looks at Darryl. "Your young friend comes too." Blackborne and Darryl follow the Islanders under the palms until they come to an open area. Racks of copra lie in the sun. To the left are island houses, low with thatched roofs and dirt floors. At the far end of the clearing is a large wooden house with a veranda and off to the right, partly hidden in the trees, is the church with a corrugated roof and a cross.

The trader Higgens comes up to Rangi and tries to lead him away until Masina steps between them. "Rangi does not work for you. He is my cousin. He works for me. He went with others to the *Tantra* and saved the copra. It is my copra. You keep away from it."

The trader huffs. "You think you can cheat me?"

"You are the cheat. You pay us little for the copra and charge too much at your store."

"I don't set the prices. Captain Blix does . . . or he did."

"Do not tell me about Captain Blix. You cheated my father with gin and promises. Where is the new copra house and the boat landing you promised? And now you try to cheat me. You did not pay for the copra and now you say it is yours, but you did not get it from *Tantra*. I did. It is my salvage." She faces the trader with her chin up, her eyes fierce. "Go, you are finished here." She waves him away. The trader looks at the others, at Rangi and Blackborne. Rangi is impassive. Blackborne smiles broadly. Darryl has never seen him simile so openly.

As the trader walks into the trees, men and women arrive, and Masina turns to talk to them. Rangi catches Blackborne's attention. "You pull the *Tantra* off the reef with your schooner." It's not a request. "We need a schooner for the copra."

"A hurricane threw *Tantra* on the reef. It will take another hurricane to get her off."

"You do not try?"

Blackborne studies him for a moment. "Only a fool would try."

Rangi looks angry, his face flush for a moment. "You come here and take but you do not give." He turns away.

Men and women wearing bright lavalavas begin to gather, the women with flowers in their hair or around their neck and the men bare chested. They sit facing each other in two lines, chatting and laughing. Masina shows Blackborne and Darryl to places at the head of the lines. Women place banana leaves before everyone and then food in the middle. Fish baked in leaves, poi, and fruit, bananas and papayas. Darryl looks down the two lines of people. They are all young, no children and no elders.

Masina sits at the head. "We did not know that you come here. Today we have only fish. Tomorrow we will have pig." She waves to the people sitting in front of her. "This is my family and friends." She turns to Blackborne. "Do you have a family on the schooner, a woman, perhaps?"

"No, just a man and a boy. Do you need a woman?"

She laughs. "No, no. I think you need a woman."

"I'm looking for a yacht called *Ariel*. Has she been here?"

"No boats come here. Only *Tantra* and now it is a wreck on the reef."

"How did it happen?"

"We have a storm three days ago and the *Tantra* dragged the anchor. We said to the captain to tie ropes to the trees on the beach but he did not do it."

"And the entire crew was drowned?"

"No. Just Captain Blix and his mate. The crew is here." She points to five islanders sitting at the far end of the line. "They do not belong here. They go back to Newtown."

"I will talk to them later."

"Good." She holds up a piece of fish. "You try this." She pops the fish into Blackborne's mouth. "You were in the storm too?"

Blackborne chews. "Yes. The storm drove us sixty miles under bare pole, pulling a drag."

"It was a bad storm. We lost many trees on the other side of the island."

"It brought us to you."

She laughs. "Yes, the good is sometimes hidden in the bad."

The sun goes down and they sit around a fire and the island people sing. Darryl is sitting near Rangi and she asks him why a priest is standing in the shadows watching them. "He is afakasi, half white man. He watches so we do not dance. He likes singing but only church singing." Rangi goes back to singing an island song.

It is late as Masina walks with Blackborne and Darryl under the trees. Before they reach the beach she stops and holds Darryl back. "Why do you wear a man's clothes?"

"The captain wants a boy."

"Ah. But that is not the way. A woman gives a man a boy."

"I am not his woman."

"No, of course not. Tomorrow we will hunt. Come talk to me later."

The beach is a pale crescent between the land and the water. Out on the lagoon the schooner floats motionless, her riding light a single point in the darkness. They say good-bye again and Darryl rows Blackborne out to the schooner. It's quiet on board. The others are asleep. Blackborne goes into the aft cabin and Darryl goes into the chart room and sits on the bunk and thinks about Masina. When her father died, she returned from Hawaiki, the main island, to take his place on the atoll. She said the whites are angry with her. "They come to my house and say I make trouble but I do not go to their house and take their copra or make them wear our lavalava or bring bad people to their house and leave them there. This is what they do, the traders and the priests and the commissioners." Darryl thought about how Blackborne watched

Masina, how he seemed drawn to her. She's beautiful and when the captain looks at her there's passion in his eyes.

DARRYL IS STILL in her bunk when Blackborne calls for a cup of coffee. She goes to the galley where Jody is setting the water to boil. "How was the party last night?"

"There's another one tonight. There will be pig this time. You and Marlin go and I'll watch the schooner."

Darryl steps carefully down the aft ladder and into the cabin where Blackborne is cleaning a rifle. "There's a feral pig on the island, an old boar that the people are afraid to go near." He wipes the rifle with a rag and puts his cleaning kit away. "They want me to hunt it. I want you to come with me."

After breakfast Darryl rows Blackborne ashore. He sits in the stern, the rifle upright between his knees. This time when they arrive at the beach, children greet them, yelling and laughing, indifferent to their nakedness as they help pull the boat onto the sand. Darryl and Blackborne walk to the village where Masina and Rangi are waiting. "Good morning Captain Andrew. You are ready to hunt?"

"Good morning." He hold up his rifle. "Yes, I am ready." Rangi glares at the rifle. There is envy beneath his haughtiness, as he grips a short spear in his right hand. Behind Masina and Rangi stands a big Islander, bigger even than Blackborne. He is naked to the waist and his hands are empty. The five of them head to the southern edge of the beach and from there they walk to where the low ridge that runs down the middle of the island falls into the sea. Rangi leads them into the jungle, keeping the ridge on their right. The sun rises higher and they walk slowly in and out of shadows. Birds call from all sides but Darryl can't see them. It's hot in the lee of the ridge and the humid air is heavy. Sweat begins to soak Darryl's shirt and run down her back. She wipes her face with her forearm and thinks of the cool breeze under the awning on the schooner.

Rangi halts, straightens up, and without making a sound, points at an opening in the jungle where the boar stands in the sunlight. In one smooth motion Blackborne raises his rifle to his shoulder and fires. The boar falls over and its legs quiver in the grass as Rangi runs in and bashes its head with his spear. No, it's not a spear, it's a pointed club. Masina claps her hands. "Good shot." They all hurry into the opening. "You shot him in the eye." Her face is shining. "You are the son of the Great Hunter." They stand over the boar, staring at it, until the big Islander bends down and grabs the boar by the fore and hind legs and throws it over his shoulders.

They start back toward the village in single file, Darryl following the Islander carrying the boar, when the sky darkens and a squall races over the ridge, pouring down rain. Masina takes Blackborne's hand and the two of them run off through the jungle, leaving the others behind. Darryl continues to follow the Islander, as rain run off the dead boar and down the Islander's naked back.

In the village Darryl sits drying in the sun, watching men dig a pit. They place stones in the bottom and then they build a fire on the stones and as the fire dies down and the stones heat up, they dress the boar, scraping the bristles from its hide. They place banana leaves on the hot stones and place the boar on the leaves and add more leaves. Women come and place breadfruit in the pit and then the men cover the pit with earth and let the boar and the breadfruit bake.

When the sun is low Blackborne and Masina come out of her house. Masina is radiant as she stands close to him. Blackborne calls Darryl and hands her his rifle. "Put this back in the locker under my bunk. Here's the key."

Darryl takes the rifle. "Yes, sir." Blackborne and Masina walk back into the house and Darryl walks to the boat and rows out to the schooner.

DARRYL IS SITTING near the helm when Jody and Marlin return late from the feast. "How was the pig?"

"It didn't taste like pig. It tasted like . . . I don't know, like wild boar." Jody grins. "Tomorrow I'm going fishing. They said there are snappers near the reef." He yawns. "I think I ate too much."

Marlin sits next to Darryl. "The captain seems taken with that island girl . . . What do you think? You think the captain is gonna do something foolish?"

"I hope not."

Marlin gets up and stands over her. "I don't like it."

"No, there's nothing to like about it." Marlin is worried. That's a bad sign.

DURING THE DAY Darryl and Marlin work on the schooner. She helps Marlin sew covers for the skylight and the forecastle hatch and then they start sewing a new fisherman staysail. Darryl sits under the awning with the canvas on her lap, watching an outrigger out on the lagoon near the reef. In the late afternoon Blackborne and Masina return from the southern islets and leave the outrigger on the beach. They weren't fishing or swimming, just floating lazily under the afternoon sun.

JODY RETURNS from the island with a load of coconuts and bananas. "The captain wants you to bring him some fresh clothes and his razor in the morning." Darryl goes below and gets out a set of Blackborne's clothes and his razor and wraps them in a clean piece of canvas and ties it with twine. In the morning she rows ashore and waits in front of Masina's house. Off to the side, standing under the palms, the priest is also waiting, a small man with a bitter face, wearing a clean but worn cassock, ragged at the edges. Since Masina has returned from Hawaiki, fewer people go to church.

Blackborne comes out of the house and Darryl hands him his clothes and the priest comes up. "I am Father Losefe. I want to talk to you. It is important." He waits but Blackborne just looks at him. The priest straightens his shoulders and tries to look assertive. "Why are you here? Masina has to marry in the church. She cannot marry you. You are not from here. You do not belong here."

"Do you have any official authority?"

"My authority is from God."

"I heard that the Captain Blix stripped you naked and whipped you through the village."

The priest spits and then crosses himself. "That spawn of the devil is in hell . . . You are like him. You come here and make trouble."

"Making trouble seems to be your job. You come here and tell the people what they can do and what they can't do."

"I do God's work."

"The Captain Blix did man's work. I'm Captain Blackborne." The priest stares, his head pushed slightly forward. "I do man's work too."

The priest's eyes widen, then he turns and scurries way between the palm trees. A coconut crab.

THE NEXT DAY Darryl rows ashore and waits for Blackborne to come out of Masina's house. A young Islander with short, black hair is also waiting. He is handsome, with very find feature, except for a nose that large and broad. He smiles at Darryl. "You wait for the captain?"

"Yes."

"You are the mate. The captain says I sail with you."

He seems too young and slender. "You were on *Tantra*. Why did the captain pick you?"

"He asks me where west is. I show him. It is night but I know where the sun goes, even at night when there are no stars to see."

Blackborne comes out of the house. He has his razor in his hand. "Dismantle the saloon table and stow it. We are going to load copra and take it to Newtown. Rangi and the crew of *Tantra* will help with the loading."

Darryl hesitates. She wants to ask why he wants to take the copra to Newtown. "Yes sir."

Blackborne points to the Islander. "This is Tane. Tell Marlin to give him a bunk."

When they get to the boat Darryl tells Tane to take the oars. He rows with long, steady strokes, seemingly without any effort. "You know how to row."

"I am an Islander. Boats are our life."

When they reach the schooner Darryl tells Marlin what Blackborne said. "This isn't a copra schooner." Marlin spits over the side.

"Marlin, we obey the captain or we get off the schooner." They go below and knock down the table and Jody moves his gear into the galley. On deck they unrig the midships awning and unbend the foresail. Rangi and the crew of *Tantra* bring the sacks of copra to the beach and Tane rows ashore and the men begin loading the copra in the schooner's boat. Darryl and

Marlin prepare the fore boom to lift the sacks out of the boat and drop them down the midships hatch. They work all day and before the sun goes down the saloon is full and the copra is onboard, some of it lashed on deck. Darryl checks the waterline. The schooner rests a little lower in the water.

The next morning they get the schooner ready for sea, but Blackborne doesn't come and they wait. Nor does he come the next day. Marlin rigs the awning over the aft cabin again and sits in the shade. "That island girl really has her hooks in him." They continue to sit under the awning as the sun goes down and the jungle turns black. Blackborne and Masina appear on the pale beach. Darryl recognizes his white shirt. They walk slowly to the south and disappear in the night. Marlin goes forward to rig the riding light on the bow.

THE SUN IS STILL BELOW the horizon as Darryl rows ashore and walks to Masina's house to wait out of sight. When Blackborne comes out and walks toward cistern, his razor in his hand, Darryl goes to the side of the house and calls softly. Masina raises the upper panel of the wall and looks at Darryl. "You said I should come and talk to you."

"Yes. But now there is nothing for you to tell me."

"About the captain?"

"About Andrew."

"Then maybe you can tell me. When is he going to sail?"

"You should sail without him." She smiles. "That is what I said. But he says no. He wants to talk to the copra traders in Newtown. He talks for me. You cannot do that."

A SQUALL PASSES through the lagoon and the wind shakes the awnings on the schooner until the heavy rain comes. Water runs off the deck and gushes out the scuppers until the squall passes to the west. When the rain stops Darryl looks at the wreck on the reef. Something isn't right. She goes below and gets the glasses and studies the wreck. The anchor chain isn't just slack, it's hanging straight down from the bow. If *Tantra* dragged her anchor, shouldn't there be some tension on the chain? Darryl puts on a pair of plastic sandals and rows across the lagoon and climbs on the reef near the bow of the wreck. She grabs the anchor chain and pulls it up hand over hand until she comes to the end. The chain broke but the last link isn't damaged. The broken link must be somewhere in the lagoon. She looks up at the deck of the wreck, almost vertical now. It has been stripped of all its rigging and gear.

Darryl rows back to the schooner where Marlin is sitting under the awning showing Tane how to splice rope. What will Marlin think of what she has found?

"A chain is only as strong as its weakest link."

"Yes. I want to see what the end in the lagoon looks like. I think I'll drag for it. Tane, you can come with me and row."

Tane rows the boat back and forth through the anchorage as Darryl drags with the boat's grapple. Now that Darryl is looking for it, she sees *Tantra's* anchor. Another pass and she hooks the chain and pulls it up to the end. Again the last link is not damaged. She holds the end of the chain in her hand and looks at the wreck on the reef. Why does everyone say she dragged her anchor? "Tane, can you dive? Can you reach the bottom here? It's five fathoms."

"You think I can bring up the anchor?"

"No." She holds up the end of the chain. "The broken link is still on the bottom. Do you think you can find it?"

"I look. But first I need something to see."

"There's a diving mask on board." Darryl checks their position before Tane rows back to the schooner.

Tane puts on the mask and dives down to the wreck's anchor. The sun shines into the lagoon and the water is clear as he swims over the bottom, following the chain. On his fourth dive he spots the link partially buried in the sand. He scoops it up and swims to the surface, holding the link above his head. Darryl takes it from him. Half a link, its two ends speckled with rust. She wipes the rust off. The ends of the link are clean and smooth. The chain didn't break. It was cut.

CHILDREN PLAY on the southern part of the beach. No one seems to go near the northern part. Before breakfast Darryl takes the boat and rows along the beach, heading north. When the beach ends at the reef, she lands the boat and walks toward the trees. Debris gathers at the high-water mark and just beyond the debris are two mounds, graves set side by side. There are no crosses or other markers but the graves look recent. She thinks she knows who is buried there. She returns to the boat and rows down along the beach past the village to where the children are playing. When she can see the cross through the trees she beaches the boat and walks toward the church. On the south side of the church is the graveyard, most of the graves have crosses. The priest comes to the door of the church, smoothing the front of his cassock with both hand. "You want to look at the church?"

"I want to know who is buried at the northern end of the beach." She points and he turns his head then looks back at Darryl.

"The captain of the *Tantra* and his mate."

"Why aren't they buried here in the church yard?"

"We bury only Christians here."

"But you would bury the island crew here . . . that is, if they had been on board *Tantra* when she wrecked on the reef?"

"What do you say?"

"Why wasn't the crew on board *Tantra*?"

"Captain Andrew sent you to ask questions?"

"Why was *Tantra* wrecked on the reef?"

The priest looks puzzled. "You think someone did that?" He becomes tense. "The hurricane came and wrecked the *Tantra*. You come here and try to make a lie." The priest walks back into his church.

THE COPRA HAS BEEN LOADED for a week when Blackborne hails the schooner. When Darryl rows ashore to fetch him there are four Islanders standing behind him. "We are taking the *Tantra* crew to New-town."

"Captain, look at this." Darryl holds up the half-link from *Tantra's* chain.

Blackborne examines it. "Where did you find this?"

"In the lagoon, near *Tantra's* anchor chain. *Tantra* didn't drag her anchor. Her chain was cut."

Blackborne hands the link back. "Show it to the commissioner in Newtown."

Darryl rows Blackborne and two Islanders out to the schooner and then sends Tane for the other two.

Blackborne stands near the helm and as soon as the anchor is aweigh, the schooner falls off and Darryl brings her up to the wind. "Hold your luff." She heads the schooner higher, watching the mainsail now as well as the pass in the reef. They sail parallel to the beach until the pass opens up, then Blackborne eases the main-sheet and Darryl turns the schooner into the pass.

When Marlin has the anchor secured on deck, Blackborne calls him aft. "Put Tane on the helm and watch him." He turns to Darryl. "Mr. Simmons, set a course for Newtown." Darryl goes down to the chart room. She has already plotted a course but she does it again. It will be an easy passage, with the wind just forward of the port beam.

The weather is fair and the Islanders eat and sleep on deck. Tane sits aft of the main-sheet, keeping an eye on a fishline he has let out, and on the second day at sea he catches a mahimahi. He cuts the fish into pieces and shows Jody how to marinate them in lime, onion, and coconut milk. On the morning of the third day they sight Hawaiki, its peaks rising above the cloud cover. The peaks are black in the distance and as they sail closer to the island the land under the peaks turns green. There are reefs along the edge of the island but there is no barrier reef and they sail close to the land until they reach the entrance to the harbor. The entrance is a long and narrow passage with high mountains on both sides that shelter it from the trade wind. Once in the passage the wind dies and the sails begin to flap. Blackborne turns on the engine and the crew lowers the sails. While Darryl is coiling the halyards she feels a wind whip down from the mountains that lie ahead of them. The schooner powers into the wind until the passage curves to the west and the harbor opens up. The harbor is landlocked, protected from the trade winds, but the high mountains make their own wind, a wind that is unpredictable and at time fierce.

In the morning Blackborne goes ashore to the harbor master and reports the wreck of the *Tantra* and the loss of her captain and mate. In the afternoon they move the schooner alongside the pier and start unloading the copra. When the trading company comes for the copra, Blackborne gives them Masina's shopping list: rice, lamp oil, knives, fish hooks and line, cotton cloth, water barrels, something for everyone on the atoll.

While waiting for the supplies to arrive, Blackborne brings the commissioner down to the pier, followed by an island policeman in a khaki uniform. Darryl steps off the schooner to meet them. "Show the commissioner the link you found."

The commissioner turns the link over in his hand. "It has been cut, probably with a hacksaw." He looks at Darryl. "You found this where?"

"In the lagoon at Manulele. *Tantra's* anchor chain was broken in half. This link was in the water near the chain."

The commissioner hands the link to the policeman. "What do you think, Semis?"

Semis studies the link. "Cut with a hacksaw." He looks up and smiles. "A case of shipwreck and murder."

"Captain Blackborne, I am unable to travel to Manulele Atoll as this time, plus there is currently no transportation available, now that the *Tantra* is a wreck." He points to the supply ship moored on the other side of the pier. "And the pass is too narrow for the *Horizon* to enter the lagoon at Manulele. However, the wreck of the *Tantra* should be looked into to see if her anchor chain was maliciously tempered with. My assistant, Officer Semis, can investigate, if you are willing to take him. It would be a great courtesy to me and the people of these islands."

Blackborne nods. "As you wish." He turns to Semis. "My supplies arrive tomorrow. We leave in the afternoon."

THEY HAVE THE WIND on the starboard quarter as they sail back to Manulele. It's a pleasant passage and Tane catches fish each day and Jody comes out of the galley and sits with Darryl during her watch. They anchor in the same place and unload the stores into the boat and row them ashore. Semis tells Tane to bring the island trader to the schooner. When Higgens climbs on deck, Blackborne leads him into the aft cabin where Semis is sitting in a deck chair with a writing pad on his lap. Blackborne sits on the bunk next to him.

Higgins looks around. "Where am I to sit?"

"You don't sit."

Semis clears his throat. "Mr. Higgens, you are the trader here on Manulele. Do you own a hacksaw?"

Higgens looks at Blackborne. "You gonna let this kanaka ask me questions?"

"I can take you on deck and let bo'sun talk to you." Higgens looks blank. "He has a whip."

"Let me begin again. Mr. Higgens, do you own a hacksaw?"

"I've got a lot of tools. I'm a trader. I sell tools."

"Can you show me your hacksaw?"

Higgens doesn't answer at first. "I lost it."

"When did you lose it?"

"I don't know."

"When did you notice it was missing?"

"After the *Tantra* wrecked." They wait. "I was suspicious. The *Tantra* could drag her anchor but she wasn't going to break her chain. Unless someone worked on it."

"Did you work on it?"

"No. Why would I do that? My copra was on her. Besides, the *Tantra* is the only trading schooner we have."

"We are not looking for a reason of the wreck. We are looking for who cut the *Tantra* chain . . . Do you have an outrigger?"

"Yes, of course. Everybody has an outrigger. This is an island for chrissakes."

"Where were you the night before the hurricane came?"

"There's always a feast after the copra is loaded."

"You were at the feast, all the time?"

"I had to fill out some papers for Captain Blix."

"And no one saw you do this?"

"I don't need anyone to watch me do my paper work."

"I think I have finished my investigation. We know who has a hacksaw and an outrigger. And you do not have an alibi." Semis turns to Blackborne. "The alibi is most important."

"Wait. I have a hacksaw and an outrigger. But that doesn't mean I used them on *Tantra's* chain." Higgens hesitates. "Question the priest. He hated Captain Blix and the mate."

"Why did you not mention the priest before?" Higgens doesn't answer. "If we question the priest, he will tell us."

Higgens shrugs. "He borrows my outrigger sometimes."

"And the hacksaw?"

"I don't know what happened to it. Maybe the priest stole it."

"You are accusing a priest, a man of God, of theft and murder?"

"He's a rascal in a cassock."

Semis turns to Blackborne. "You have a place to put Mr. Higgens?"

Blackborne leads Higgens up to the foredeck and points to the forecastle hatch. "Stay down there."

112

"That kanaka policeman means to get me hanged."

"That's how it looks."

Higgens' face turns red. "This is not how a white man is treated. You should know that."

"Higgens, as long as you are in my schooner you are my guest but that doesn't mean I have to like it. Get down in the fo'c'sle."

WHEN BLACKBORNE LEADS the priest into the aft cabin, Semis stands and gives the priest his chair. "Father Losefe, your name has been mentioned during my investigation into the wreck of the *Tantra*. I hope you understand that this a formality, but the wreck of the *Tantra* is a very serious case and it is my duty to ask you a few questions."

Losefe nods. "Yes, the wreck of the *Tantra* was most unfortunate."

"Do you own a hacksaw?"

"I do not. I am a priest not a worker."

"Yes, of course. Do you own an outrigger?"

"I do not. The people here are kind enough to take me in their outriggers wherever I need to go."

"Yes, of course. The night before the hurricane there was a feast. Were you there?"

"Yes, it is my duty to see that there is no backsliding during these feasts, especially when the traders are there. They give out gin, even though it is forbidden."

"So you were there the entire time."

"It was a Saturday, so toward the end of the feast I left to prepare for Sunday services."

"Yes, of course." Semis turns to Blackborne. "I think that's everything."

"If we are finished, a member of my parish is ill. I should like to go visit him."

"Yes, of course. They will take you ashore." The priest stands and climbs on deck. "Captain Blackborne, I would like to return with my prisoner to Newtown as soon as possible."

"Mr. Simmons." Darryl comes out of the chart room where she has been listening. "As soon as Tane returns with the boat, set sail for Newtown."

"You are not coming?"

"It's time you had command." He smiles. "It's an easy passage to Newtown and back."

Darryl and Blackborne climb on deck. "The priest had a motive for wrecking *Tantra*, Higgens didn't."

"The people on the island want to get rid of Higgens." Darryl looks away from him. This is the first time she hears the captain say something false. It must be that woman, Masina. The captain is dallying

114

with her and forgetting about everything else, including the woman he has been chasing.

DARRYL STANDS AT THE HELM and looks down the deck of the schooner. Is everything ready? The boat is on board and the gaskets are off. During the mutiny, when she sailed the schooner alone, she didn't have time to think about running the schooner. She just had time to act and hope and nothing else. Now she has time to think. Marlin is at the mainmast, watching her. Does he trust her? He doesn't like the off-handed way the captain gave her command. She can't help it. She scans the horizon for squalls one more time and then she nods for Marlin and Tane to raise the mainsail. Marlin goes forward and starts the anchor winch and then sets the staysail. Once the anchor breaks ground, the schooner falls off and gains way. Darryl heads her up and the schooner glides through the calm water of the lagoon. Short-handed but the maneuver was smooth. Once on the open sea, everything will be easy. Maybe she will like this after all.

Semis isn't any help with the schooner but he expects to be served. He calls for his food to be brought to him in the aft cabin. When he wants coffee he goes into the galley and tells Jody and then returns to the aft cabin and waits for Jody to bring it. In the afternoon he shackles Higgens to the main shrouds.

"Officer Semis, I don't want Higgens there. Take him to the fo'c'sle."

"It is not for you to say." Semis goes into the aft cabin and lies down in a bunk.

In the evening Jody brings Higgens his supper and holds the plate while Higgens eats with his free hand. Semis comes out of the aft hatch and looks at Jody and Higgens and then he turns and looks at Darryl at the helm. "Where is my dinner?"

"Officer Semis, I am in command of this schooner. Take your prisoner to the fo'c'sle."

On the morning of the third day at sea they sight Hawaiki with dark clouds swirling like smoke around its peaks. They sail through the entrance of the long passage that leads to the harbor, and as soon as the hills rise up on both sides, the wind fails. When Darryl tries to start the engine, the starter grinds but the engine doesn't catch. The schooner loses way and begins to drift with her bow pointing toward the western shore, a sheer cliff face. Darryl watches the shore. There's an ebb, slowly carrying the schooner back out to sea. Up ahead the water ripples, turning dark as wind sweeps down the passage. A blast hits the schooner and the main boom jerks up, breaking the bail on the main-sheet as the sail catches the wind. Darryl brings the schooner up until the sails shiver and Marlin gets a rope on the main boom. Darryl helps him secure the boom and then she lets the schooner falls off the wind. The schooner picks speed and begins racing toward the shore. Darryl brings her about and heads the schooner for the other shore. The wind continues to gust as they tack up the narrow passage, until they reach the far end and the wind lets up and they drift into the harbor.

THE NEXT AFTERNOON Tane rows Darryl out to the schooner and they climb aboard and Darryl goes up to Marlin. "They couldn't repair the old bail so they made a new one." She hands Marlin the bail. "I can't get an engineer until next week, but Tane says he wants to have a look at the engine." Darryl opens the hatch behind the mainmast and she and Tane climb down into the engine room.

Tane looks through the tool box and takes out a wrench. "I clean the filter." He loosens the fuel filter and lowers it and its casing into a bucket. He lifts out the filter and looks in the casing. "Too much water." He dumps the contents in the bucket and mounts the filter again. "You can start the engine." The stater motor grinds at first and then the engine catches. The engine sounds normal.

Darryl and Tane look at each other and smile. "Very good. You are the engineer, at least until the captain comes back aboard." They climb out of the engine room. "Marlin, raise the anchor. We'll move over to the pier and fill our water tanks."

Once they are alongside the pier, Darryl sends Jody and Tane to buy flour. They return with a push cart loaded with supplies, flour, potatoes, carrots, onions, and a case of jam. "I didn't give you enough money to buy all that."

"The storekeeper is right behind us. You can pay him."

Semis walks down the pier waving something. "This is a letter for Father Losefe." He hands Darryl the letter.

"I'll see that he gets it."

"You must do that." Semis pivots and walks back up the pier.

THE SCHOONER SAILS through the night and into the dawn. Jody walks aft, bringing Darryl a cup of coffee. He is not frightened of the sea but he is wary, as if a wave is waiting to catch him on deck. Darryl takes the coffee and surveys the horizon already visible in

118

the weak morning light. When the sun rises and light spreads over the ocean, she can see Manulele Atoll. Tane climbs aloft and later when he returns to the deck he points at the southern islets. "The birds have come." Darryl uses the glasses. The petrels have returned to the islets to breed and as the schooner sails through the pass they can hear the cry of birds above the sound of the breaking surf.

They anchor in the same place and Darryl goes ashore to see Blackborne. He's not at Masina's house, so she walks over to the church to deliver Losefe's letter. It's Sunday and as she approaches the church, she can hear Losefe preaching. She looks in a window. He is preaching in the island language, mainly to women and a few old men. The people sit passively until the singing starts then they come alive, standing and singing so loud they drown out Losefe's voice. Darryl waits outside until the service is over and everyone has left the church. Losefe comes out and glares at Darryl, "I have a letter for you, from Newtown." She holds it out.

Losefe takes the letter and looks at it carefully. "I have waited for this." He holds out his hand. "Thank you very much indeed." Darryl shakes his hand. It's smooth and soft. The hand has never held a hacksaw, or any other tool.

DARRYL FINDS TANE in the galley talking to Jody about going fishing. "Tane, come with me. I want to talk to you." Darryl leads Tane to the aft cabin. "Sit on the bunk."

"You sit too?"

"Tane, why weren't you on *Tantra* during the hurricane?"

"We have a feast after loading the copra. Captain Blix and the mate do not come to the feast. They stay on board their schooner and drink gin."

"So you weren't warned that something was going to happen to *Tantra*?"

"No. We are not warned and not surprised."

"Not surprised? What do you mean?"

"I tell you. Two days before the hurricane, Rangi takes Masina in his outrigger to the *Tantra*. Masina wants to talk to Captain Blix about the copra. She does not like the trader and she wants a better price."

"Masina wanted to cut Higgens out of the copra trade."

"Yes, I think that. But Captain Blix does not talk to Masina. He says he does not talk to kanaka women. I see Masina is very angry, but she leaves and gets back in the outrigger. Then Captain Blix does something very bad. He lets the dirty water out of the schooner."

"The bilge water?"

"Yes. And the dirty water splashes on the outrigger and on Masina and Rangi."

"You saw this?"

"Yes. Captain Blix and the mate laugh. We do not laugh. It is a very bad thing they do."

THE NIGHT IS CLEAR and the waning moon shows Blackborne and Masina walking on the beach. Jody comes on deck and sits next to Darryl. "What are you looking at?"

"The captain and Masina are walking together." She points.

"We can go for a walk too. We can take the boat to the other end of the beach." Darryl walks over to Tane sitting on the forecastle hatch and tells him they are taking the boat for a little while. Darryl rows toward the northern end of the beach and they climb out and pull the boat up on the sand. "The captain and Masina are holding hands."

"Yes."

"You don't want to hold hands?"

"We are just taking a walk, Jody."

"You don't think we can be more than just friends."

"We are more than just friends. We are best friends." It's not what he means of course but Jody was more like a brother to her than anything else. She can't help it if he doesn't see it that way. "When did you know I was a girl?"

"I've always known . . . I knew it when you led me off the *Holiday.*"

"Jody, what's important to you?"

"You are important to me."

"Besides me. What do you want to be?"

"I don't know. I don't think I'm old enough to know that."

"You are the same age I am." They stop walking. "What's important to me is being mate of the *Ellie.* I don't want anything to change that."

"You can't love the schooner the way you love a person."

"Of course not. The schooner is not a person. It's a way of life. Let's go back."

WITH THE CAPTAIN spending his time with Masina, Darryl decides the crew needs to stop sitting around. "Marlin, what do you think about painting the topsides?"

"We could do that." He looks up into the rigging. "Or we can start with the topmasts."

Darryl carries the bull rope aloft and rigs it and once the rope takes the weight of the topmast, she drives out the fid in the heel and lowers the topmast down to the deck. Marlin sets up two sawhorses and they lay the topmast on them. The mast is dry and Darryl oils it with linseed oil and Marlin sands and paints the white masthead. While the topmast dries, Darryl gets out the bo'sun chair, hoists herself to the crosstrees and then slowly lowers herself again, oiling the mainmast as she goes down. When she is done with the mainmast she tells Tane to send down the fore topmast.

Marlin smiles at her. "You had to do it yourself first, didn't you?"

"Isn't that the way the captain does it?"

The next morning they send the topmasts aloft and start scraping and sanding the taffrail. They work forward along the gunwale until they reach the bow. Darryl sends Tane out on the bowsprit to sand it. "What do you think, Marlin? One undercoat and two coats of gloss?"

"We should cover those bare spots first."

They start on the topside next, one holding the boat in place and the other two cleaning off the engine soot and the rust coming off the chain plates. One evening, after applying the second coat of gloss on the topsides, Marlin and Tane sit with Darryl near the helm drinking coffee. "What do you think, Marlin? We clean the paint locker and the lazaret next."

"Not much work there. It's time to clean the bilge."
That's how they spent the days waiting for Blackborne
to return to the schooner.

THE SEASON CHANGES from dry to wet and the days
become clouded and it rains heavily in the afternoons.
A squall sweeps in from the east, rushing over the reef
but not reaching the lagoon. When the squall passes
and the horizon clears, a ketch sails through the pass
and anchors next the schooner.

"You wanna go over and talk to them?"

"You go, Marlin. Take Tane." After few minutes
Marlin returns to the schooner. "The ketch is called
Orion. There are three of them on board, two men
and a woman. They are yelling at each other so we
didn't stay."

"Where did they come from?"

"From the west. The captain will wanna talk to
them." The crew of *Orion* lowers the dinghy in the
water and rows ashore. Darryl follows them in the
schooner's boat. As she pulls the boat on the beach
she can hear the two men arguing. When she looks
up they are starting to fight, pushing and then punch-
ing each other.

The woman from *Orion* walks over to Darryl. "Hi,
are you from the schooner? Do you need a crew?

I want to get off the *Orion*." She points to the men fighting. "Those two yell at each other all the time. Now look at them. It's crazy."

The woman looks a little older and a little stronger than Darryl. Her hair is an unruly dark blonde and she doesn't tan easily. "We can use one more crew but I'll have to talk to the captain first."

"Great. I've been on the *Orion* for three months and I'm fed up with the yelling and fighting. You know what they're fighting about now? Who ate the last jar of orange marmalade. It's just crazy."

"Have you seen any other yachts lately?"

"No, not really. We've been sailing through the atolls to the west. Many of them are uninhabited. On one of them there was a boat on the beach. All her gear was gone and there was no one around."

"Was it a sloop called *Ariel?*"

"How did you know that? Have you been there too?"

"We are looking for her."

"Well, like I said, she was abandoned."

"I'm Darryl. What's your name?"

"Arabella. Everyone calls me Bella."

"Come with me and I'll introduce you to the captain of the *Ellie*."

The two men exhaust themselves and go off in separate directions. Darryl leads Bella to the village where Blackborne and Masina are sitting on the veranda of Masina's house.

"Captain, this is Bella. She just arrived on a ketch from the west. They found *Ariel* abandoned on an atoll."

Blackborne jumps up and takes Bella's arm and leads her off to the side. After a few minutes he abruptly turns to Darryl. "Where is the rest of the crew?"

"One is walking toward the church. The other one is on the beach, walking north." Blackborne heads for the church.

Bella looks surprised. "What is going on? He didn't say if I could join you."

"Do you know the name of the atoll where you found *Ariel*?"

"It's a small atoll. I'm not sure it had a name."

IN THE EVENING Blackborne comes aboard the schooner and calls for Darryl. "Mr. Simmons, we will careen on the beach, north of the village." He points. "The next high tide is at 22:00."

"Yes, sir."

"Are the water tanks full?"

"Yes, sir. I filled them in Newtown."

"Good. Get the schooner ready while it's still light."

After Marlin and Tane prepare a stern anchor, they eat dinner and then wait, sitting on the cabin top. There is no moon but they can see the pale beach. Blackborne starts the engine and Marlin starts the anchor winch. Darryl heads the schooner toward the beach. "More to port." Blackborne looks aft. "Away the stern anchor." The schooner gently strikes the sand. "Swing the booms out to port." As the tide runs out the schooner leans over on her port side. "Mr. Simmons, set a watch on the beach." Blackborne climbs off the schooner and walks toward the village.

They start cleaning the starboard bottom while it is still dark. Darryl holds a kerosine lamp as Marlin and Tane scrap the sea growth off the hull. "Damn, that's some really poor paint we got in Portville." The after-half of the hull is still in the water at low tide and they splash about as they clean toward the stern.

While they are eating breakfast on the beach, Blackborne arrives and examines the hull. Darryl walks up and stands to next him. "We could use another crew member. Bella, the woman from *Orion*, asked if we could take her on."

"I don't want a woman on the schooner."

As the sun rises higher, Marlin hauls the booms to midships and then they wait in the shade of the palm trees. When the schooner is upright, Marlin eases the booms to starboard and when the tide runs out, the schooner begins to lie on her starboard side. They scrap the port side in the late afternoon and then sit under the palm trees, waiting for the tide to turn.

"Mr. Simmons, if I'm not back in time for the tide, get the schooner off the beach. We'll leave as soon as I come aboard in the morning."

"Yes, sir . . . Where are we heading."

"We are going west, to an atoll called Epang."

The schooner is upright and when Blackborne doesn't arrive, Darryl starts the engine and puts it in reverse. "Start the winch." The winch whines, pulling on the stern anchor. The schooner doesn't move. Darryl pushes the throttle down. The drive shaft shudders and the schooner slowly slips into the lagoon. The island appears as a low shadow in the night and the surf on the reef is a thin white line. "Marlin, set the main anchor and then take in the stern anchor. I don't know how long we will have to wait."

Darryl climbs on deck at first light. *Orion* is gone. She drinks coffee, waiting for Blackborne. Why isn't he coming? He wasn't like this before, hardly staying in one place longer than a few days. The sun rises above the clouds that ring the horizon. She sees Bella on the beach and rows ashore. "They left me behind. They took me ashore and then they left. What am I going to do?" The panic in Bella's voice makes Darryl hesitate.

"I'm going to see Captain Blackborne now. We'll be leaving soon, so wait here by our boat." Darryl walks to the village.

Rangi is sitting on the steps of Masina's veranda. "You do not come here."

"I want to see Captain Blackborne?"

"He is not here."

"Where is he?"

"He is not here."

"Where is Masina? I want to talk to her."

"You do not come here." He waves her away.

Darryl walks through the village looking in the open doorways of the huts and asking, "Captain Blackborne?" The people appear shy and do not look at her as they shake their heads. She walks over to the church and goes inside.

Losefe comes in behind her. "You want something?"

"I'm looking for Captain Blackborne. Have you seen him this morning?"

"He is not here."

"Yes, I can see that. Do you know where he is?"

"Look somewhere else."

"Where?"

Losefe sweeps his arm to include the entire island. "Look out there."

What does he mean? "Has something happened to Captain Blackborne?"

"Find him and you will know. Leave here now."

Darryl begins to search the island. She walks along the beach from the northern end near the two graves to the southern end, opposite the islets where the petrels are breeding. She returns to the boat on the beach where Bella is waiting. "What did the captain say?"

"I haven't seen him yet." She is not sure what to do next. "Get your bag and come with me to the schooner." They climb aboard and Darryl calls for Marlin. "Something has happened. Captain Blackborne is missing." Marlin stares at her. "We have to search the island. Two of us. Me and Tane. You keep watch on the schooner. Don't let anyone from the island on board."

"This comes from mixing with these people. Doesn't he know that not every couple is a pair?"

Darryl takes Tane and returns to the island. "Go to the village and talk to the people. See if they know anything."

"I am not from here. They do not trust me."

"They trust me even less, plus I can't even talk to them."

Tane walks toward the village and Darryl walks to Higgens house and checks it before heading to the southern edge of the island. She looks at the islets covered with nesting petrels. She may have to search there but not yet. When she comes to the ridge that runs down the middle of the island she walks through the jungle, keeping the ridge on her right. She has been here before. Up ahead is the opening where the captain shot the wild boar. She picks up her pace until she reaches the opening. On the other side is a mound. Someone is buried here. She uses her hands to uncover one end and finds a head wrapped in canvas. She takes out her knife and makes a slit in the canvas. It's the captain, his eyes are open. She tries to close them but they don't stay closed. She folds the canvas over and puts a rock on it to hold it together and covers the head again. She sits back on her haunches, her arms resting on her knees, and looks up in the trees where the birds are hiding. There's a pressure behind her eyes. Slowly she takes in what has happened. She is responsible now. For everything. She stands and looks around. She hears a buzzing and her head feels heavy. Which way is back to the boat?

Darryl walks through the jungle, stumbling in the underbrush. When she reaches to the beach Tane is waiting. "No one in the village talks to me." She stares at him. What is he saying? "We go to the schooner now?" She looks at the schooner. There is something wrong. The anchor is too short. Marlin has to let out more chain.

"Yes. I'll row you out." Darryl sits on the middle thwart and takes the oars and stares at the island. Why is it so quiet?

"What happened to your knee. Did you fall?"

She looks at her knee. Blood is running down her shin. Yes, she fell twice, maybe three times. She looks back at the island. She can't see the house where that woman lives, that woman who should have killed herself instead of the captain. The boat drifts back to the beach and bumps up against the sand.

"Maybe I row now?"

Darryl looks at the oars in her hands. "Yes. You row now."

Darryl climbs aboard the schooner and holds on to the main shrouds. This is the world she knows.

She wants to leave, to set a course and sail away. But there's something she has to do first. Marlin is sitting near the helm. "Captain Blackborne is dead."

"Are you sure . . . What happened?"

"Have Jody bring me a coffee." Marlin hesitates and then goes below. Jody brings her a cup of coffee and she sits near the helm sipping, not looking at anything. When the cup is empty she looks up at Marlin. "Can you make a coffin?"

"A coffin? Are you sure he's dead?"

"He's buried in the jungle, where he shot the wild boar. I uncovered his face. His eyes are still open."

Marlin sits on the cabin top and takes off his hat. "He was a good man . . . You want to take him to Newtown?"

"I want to bury him here, where he died."

"I can setup a workbench on deck."

"Set it up on the beach. You can use wood from Higgens' house."

"You want the people on the island see me make a coffin?"

"Yes, I want them to watch. Make the coffin and we'll fetch Captain Blackborne and bury him next to Captain Blix and his mate."

Bella walks aft to Darryl and Marlin. "Where can I put my gear?"

They look at Bella for a moment until the mundane world comes back into focus. "Marlin, show Bella a bunk in the saloon and where she can stow her gear." They start forward. "Wait. What's your full name?"

"Arabella Lawrence." Darryl goes below to the chart room. She logs the death of Captain Blackborne and then signs Bella on.

Marlin sets up a workbench on the beach, two sawhorses and a heavy plank. Marlin and Tane walk to the trader's house and pull its veranda apart and carry the planks to the beach. Marlin doesn't have any nails, just screws, so he has to bore holes to put the screws in. Each time he bores a hole he says, "He was a good man."

Darryl keeps watch on the schooner. Except for Marlin and Tane, she can't see anyone on the island, but the people are there and they are watching. Losefe comes down to the beach and tries to talk to Marlin but Marlin ignores him, so he turns to Tane. They talk and then Losefe walks away shaking his head. Now the people will know what the big box is for.

When the coffin is ready, they have to get the body from the jungle. Darryl doesn't like leaving the schooner without Marlin on board, but Marlin will want to bring the body back and she has to show him where it is. They find a handcart behind Higgens' house and drag it through the village and into the jungle. When they reach the opening, they use their hands to remove the dirt from the body and then brush off the canvas. The canvas is stained around the head. Darryl places a hand under the neck and lifts the head. With her other hand she feels the back of the head. It's soft. The skull has been crushed. She lowers the head and opens the slit she cut and places two coins over Blackborne's eyes and then sews the slit closed.

Marlin sits back on his haunches. "Don't you want to see how he died?"

"I know how he died." They place the body on the cart and pull it back through the jungle. When they reach the village they rest. No one is about. The people have hidden themselves or they have run away. Darryl and Marlin pull the cart along the edge of the beach, where the ground is firm, until they reach the two graves. The coffin is already there but they forgot a shovel. Marlin goes back to Higgens' house to look for one. They dig until water begins to seep into the grave. It's not very deep but it's enough to cover the coffin.

"I can make a cross."

"There isn't time, Marlin. I want to get away from this island."

"Are you gonna say a few words?"

Darryl looks down at the grave. "We commit this body to the ground, earth to earth."

Marlin nods. "Earth to earth, ashes to ashes, dust to dust . . . He was a good man."

When Darryl arrives at Masina's house, Rangi stops her at the veranda. "You do not come here."

"Masina will see me."

Masina comes out, her eyes red and her shoulders sagging. She is wearing Blackborne's gold wedding band on her thumb. She waves Rangi into the house.

"He wanted to leave me."

"He would have come back."

"He wanted to go to his wife."

"Captain Blackborne would not want a woman who didn't want him. He wanted to see her. He wanted her to tell him why she left." Masina doesn't believe this. "He wanted to show her that she made a mistake. It was his revenge. He wasn't above that." Masina stares at her before lowering her head. "You didn't kill him but you made Rangi think you wanted him dead, just like you made Rangi think you wanted Captain Blix dead. Captain Blackborne was just another white man to Rangi."

Rangi comes out of the house. "You go now."

Masina turns to go in the house. "Wait. Give me the ring."

"No. It is all I have."

"It's bad luck to wear someone else's wedding ring."

"I do not believe it."

"Don't you know? It's cursed."

Masina hesitates and then pulls off the ring and throws it down. "You take it."

Darryl picks up ring from the veranda floor and holds it up. "It's a wife's curse."

Masina begins to wail as she runs into the house.

Darryl walks through the palms to the beach. She can still hear Masina. It's grief, maybe even despair. The captain believed in consequences. When she reaches the three graves she looks at the name engraved inside the ring: Eleanor. He named the schooner after her? Maybe the ring is cursed. She makes a small hole in Blackborne's grave and drops the ring in and then covers it up.

When she returns to the boat on the beach, Rangi is waiting for her.

"You leave tomorrow when the sun is there." He points to ten o'clock in the eastern sky. "I bring fruit, coconuts and bananas to the schooner."

"Tomorrow then." Darryl rows out to the schooner.

THEY ALL SIT around the table in the saloon. Jody and Tane caught some snappers earlier in the day and now they eat silently. Nobody asks what is next or when they are leaving or where they are going. Once in a while Jody glances at Darryl at the head of the table.

Later Darryl sits on the starboard bunk in the aft cabin, still the captain's cabin as she thinks of it. She's tired but not sleepy. She goes in the chart room and looks at the chart. She has studied it before. Epang Atoll doesn't appear on the chart. It should be there. Either it has another name or it's so small it's just a speck on the paper. She lies in her bunk. Something is wrong but she doesn't know what it is. It's a bad feeling and it won't let her sleep. The ship's clock strikes eight bells. 0400. She goes on deck. There is still a fire at the center of the village. Rangi and his friends are awake. What are they doing? Then she knows. They are waiting, getting ready. It's the schooner.

She goes forward and into the saloon and wakes Jody and Bella. "Quiet. Don't turn on the lights." She goes in the forecastle and wakes Marlin and Tane. "No lights. Come on deck." The crew assembles near the mainmast. "We are getting underway now, but quietly. Marlin and Tane, bring the boat around to the other side of the schooner and hoist it on board. Bella, help me unrig the awning." The tenseness in her voice makes them obey without questioning. Bella folds the awning and carries it forward and Darryl throws the gaskets off the mainsail. She looks to the south. The birds on the islets are quiet.

Shadows move under the palm trees where the outriggers lie on the beach. "Start the anchor winch. Tane, Bella raise the main." Darryl ducks down into the aft cabin and gets out the rifle under the bunk and pulls open the bolt. It's loaded. She doesn't have time to look for more cartridges. She goes back on deck and leans the rifle in the steering well. Men on the island are dragging outriggers to the water. Marlin gestures from the foredeck. The anchor is aweigh. He sets the staysail and Darryl lets the schooner fall off to gather way. Tane looks at her. "Set the foresail and jib, then help Marlin secure the anchor." The outriggers are paddling toward them, five of them with four men in each one. Darryl is surprised at how fast they move. She lets go of the wheel and checks that the schooner holds her course and then she takes up the rifle, faces aft, and fires two rounds over the heads of the men in the outriggers.

Bella comes up behind her. "You're aiming high."

"I'm not trying to hit anyone." She points the rifle at the lead outrigger. It's close enough for her to recognize Rangi. She fires another round and water splashes against the outrigger. The men stop paddling and the other outriggers come up and stop next to it.

Darryl looks at the pass, drops the rifle in the steering well and eases the main-sheet. The schooner heals over, gaining speed as she heads into the pass. Tane is in the crosstrees setting the topsail. The flying jib is set and Marlin is getting the fisherman staysail ready to hoist. The schooner clears the pass and Darryl looks back. The outriggers haven't moved. Tane returns to the deck and helps Marlin set the fisherman. As the sun rises above the horizon, the schooner heads away from the atoll.

Marlin comes aft. "What did they want?"

"They wanted the schooner."

Captain

DARRYL STEERS the schooner west, letting Manulele Atoll fall astern. The white surf on the reef stretches to a thin line and the bright jungle fades into the low clouds on the horizon. She sends the crew below for breakfast. "When you are finished eating I'll set the watch." The crew is below longer than usual, taking time over their coffee. When they return to the deck the crew gathers at the helm, even Jody who rarely leaves the galley. Darryl looks at them as they wait for her to speak. "Captain Blackborne is dead."

"It was murder. Masina did it, didn't she?"

Darryl expected Marlin to speak up, not Jody. "I don't have any evidence against Masina. Going to the commissioner in Newtown will only cause us problems, problems we don't need at this time."

"That's not right."

"Jody, getting one of us, or probably all of us, accused of mutiny and murder isn't justice either." The crew is quiet, looking down at the deck.

Marlin speaks up. "So where are we heading?"

"We are heading for the atoll where *Orion* found *Ariel.* It's what Captain Blackborne wanted." They are uneasy. "And it's what I want."

"But we . . ."

"This cruise isn't finished until we find *Ariel* and Eleanor Blackborne, the owner of this schooner. It's what we have to do. I think you can all see that." She looks at them, one after the other. "Marlin, you have the first watch. Bella come with me to the chart room." A chart of the western half of the Southern Ocean is lying on the chart table. "Can you point out Epang Atoll on the chart?"

"No . . . I can't read a chart."

Is that why *Orion* left her behind? She's incompetent? "Can you steer a compass course?"

"Of course. But your compass doesn't have any numbers."

"Marlin will show you how to use it. Ask Tane to come here." Tane comes into the chart room. "Can you point out Epang Atoll on the chart?"

Tane studies the chart. He points to two nameless specks. "How far is this from Manulele?"

144

Darryl picks up the dividers and measures the distance. "About six hundred miles."

"Six, maybe seven days. Epang is one of these, the one in the southeast." He looks up. "You show me how to uses that?" He points to the dividers.

Darryl places the plotter on the chart and draws the course. "Yes, but first tell Marlin to steer West-by-Northwest."

A CHANGE IN THE MOTION of the schooner wakes Darryl. The schooner is off course. She looks at the clock. A quarter to midnight. Bella's watch. When Darryl climbs on deck, stamping up the ladder, Bella's head snaps up. Bella looks at the compass and starts bringing the schooner back on course. Darryl sits next to her on the steering box. "Trouble staying awake?"

"Yeah. I'm not used to it. I didn't steer at night on *Orion.*"

"No? I can take your night watch if you help Jody in the galley."

"What do I have to do?"

"Clean up mainly. Clear the table after meals, sweep below deck, and clean the head."

Bella wrinkles her nose. "That sounds like servant's work."

"We all serve on *Ellie*. We all do what we can. It's the only way to keep the schooner running."

"I want to work on deck."

"Good. Your watch is almost over, go wake Tane." She watches Bella go forward. Is she ever going to be of any use on board?

Darryl likes the feel of the schooner with the wind on the quarter. When the waves pass under her, the counter lifts and the schooner slides down their face, gaining a little more speed as she rolls to leeward. Tane comes aft, smiling because he likes standing watch. "Wake me when you come off watch. I want to show you something."

Darryl goes below, climbs in her bunk and immediately falls asleep and then Tane is in the chart room waking her. "What do you want to show me?"

"How many knots are we making?"

"It says six knots."

"This is the ship's log." She opens the logbook. "I want you to write up your watch each time you come off watch. Time, course, knots, wind, and any changes that occur." She hands him a pen. He looks at the previous entry and then begins writing. He has a neat hand, the letters small but clear. "The logbook helps us keep track of our dead reckoning position."

"I mark our position on the chart too?"

146

"It's not necessary. Only if we have a course change." Tane puts the pen down. "Write your initials at the end of your entry."

"I write Tane."

"What is your full name?"

"I am Tane Palamo, like my father."

"Turn to the front of the logbook and write your name on the crew list. I forgot to do it earlier."

Darryl wants to show him the almanac but she decides not to rush him. She lets the logbook and dead reckoning sink in first.

After writing his name Tane studies the crew list. "Only Marlin from the first crew." He looks up at Darryl. "This is an unlucky boat?"

"No. It's just that a good crew is hard to find."

"A good captain, too?" He smiles at her.

"Tane, you can joke with me but only as long as you obey me."

Darryl goes on deck and sits next to Marlin. "Can you get Bella to help you with repairing the ratlines?"

"Sure. You want to see if she is afraid of heights?"

"She wants to work on deck. Have her help you whenever you can. She has a lot to learn."

They sit quietly watching the sky clear in the predawn. Darryl waits for Marlin to speak. "Why are we going after *Ariel?* The people on *Orion* said Eleanor Blackborne isn't there anymore."

"Where do you want to go Marlin? Back to Newtown or Portville?"

"No. There is no sense in going back to those places."

"Captain Blackborne gave this cruise a purpose. He's dead now but the purpose is still with us. If we give up his purpose we have to come up with something else. We can't just sit at anchor in some lagoon. We have to sail. We have to go somewhere. Where do you want to go?"

Marlin thinks for a while. "There are a lot of islands out there." He waves his arm at the horizon where the stars disappeared. "We could have a look at some of them."

"Marlin, that's what we are doing."

DARRYL WAKES in her bunk. It's dark. Someone is in the chart room. "Jody?"

Jody is sitting on the edge of her bunk. "I have to tell you something. Bella visits me at night."

Darryl sits up. She can see the outline of his head. "You want me to talk to her?"

"What for?"

"You like her to visit you?"

"Of course. I just want you to know . . . Is it okay?"

"Yes. Just try to be discreet."

"Are you jealous?"

"No. I don't want Bella to visit me."

Jody's laugh sounds like a snicker. "She thinks you are a boy but she likes me better."

DARRYL CHECKS TANE's chart work. Seventy-six miles to Epang Atoll, they should sight it tomorrow. She goes into the aft cabin and looks in the lockers under Blackborne's bunk. The first locker contains ammunition for the rifle, an air foghorn, and a wooden box. She takes out the box and opens it. A flare gun, brass with a wooden handle, and an assortment of flares. The second locker, she knows, contains the captain's clothes. She pulls out the drawer under the vanity and finds a photograph of a young woman. She holds the photograph up to the light. The woman is wearing a dark cotton dress with short sleeves and open neck. Darryl can't tell the color of her eyes but they are light, blue or gray. Her hair is also light. She is slim and beautiful and looks mischievous. Darryl turns the photograph over. Nora, no date. She looks through the drawer but doesn't find any more photographs. She takes up the photograph again. How old is the photograph? The young woman is little more than a school girl. Why would the captain keep such a photograph? Darryl looks out a starboard porthole. The sea is dark blue and the white caps are brilliant in the noon sun. Masina is also young and beautiful.

THE NEXT DAY in the late afternoon Marlin sights the dark line of Epang Atoll. Tane goes aloft. As the sun falls toward the horizon, the dark line rises up and they can see the white surf that marks the barrier reef, and behind it, the palm trees with their green heads swaying in the breeze. When the sun drops below the horizon and the atoll disappears in the night, Tane returns to the deck. "I see a boat on the beach. It is a yacht without a mast."

"We'll heave-to and wait for morning. Can you see the pass?"

"Yes. It is small, maybe too small and the wind blows in. We cannot sail out such a pass."

"We'll take the boat in after breakfast."

The morning is gray as they put the boat over the side. Tane rows into the narrow pass and lifts the oars as the wind drives the boat through and into the light-green lagoon. Tane beaches the boat next to the yacht lying on her port side. Darryl walks around the yacht, a sloop named *Ariel*, her deck stripped of sails and running rigging. Tane stands next to Darryl. "When the western Islanders see a boat on the beach, they think it is theirs and they take everything. But this was not Islanders. See? They did not take the brass." He points to the life-line stanchions.

"So what do you think? White men who need sailing gear? That suggests a sailboat that has been out in these islands a long time. What kind of boat is that?"

"Blackbirder."

"Blackbirder? A sailboat that recruits laborers?"

"They do not recruit them. They steal them."

Darryl looks around the beach. "Eleanor Blackborne didn't leave the island herself. Her dinghy is still here. She must have gone with the blackbirders, if that is what they are." Darryl begins to look around the camp. There's a fire pit but no shelter. They must have slept on the sloop. She walks into the trees and in a few minutes she reaches the other side of the island. Too small to support human habitation. She walks back toward the sloop, circling around until she discovers a grave. She studies it for a moment and then uncovers one end. A foot. She covers it back up and uncovers the other end. The head of a man with pale hair, and eyes washed out like a dead fish. She brushes more sand away. There's an old scar on the jaw. She covers up the head again and returns to the beach.

Tane is holding up something. A spent cartridge. "Where did you find it?"

"There, by the fire pit."

"Stay here." She walks back to the grave and uncovers the body. It has been in the ground for a while and she doesn't like doing it but she needs to know. The dead man's blue shirt is covered in dried blood and in the center of the left pocked is a small hole where the blood came from. The man, whoever he was, Eleanor Blackborne's lover perhaps, was shot in the chest.

Darryl goes back to the yacht on the beach and steps in the cockpit and climbs below. The cabin is neat and clean, bunks made, dishes and clothes put away. She opens the drawer under the navigation table and takes out the logbook. The last entry describes the hurricane. It caught them anchored in the lagoon and threw the sloop on the beach, breaking her mast. Nothing about how long they were on the atoll or how Eleanor Blackborne left it. Darryl flips to the front of the logbook, no crew list.

As Tane rows Darryl back across the lagoon, a squall catches them and they lose sight of the pass until the sky clears again. The wind blows hard through the pass and Darryl helps Tane row against it as the water from the squall drips off them and gathers in the bottom of the boat.

Marlin and Bella are waiting near the mainmast as Darryl and Tane climb aboard. "Marlin, what is the name of Eleanor Blackborne's lover?"

"Giles. Giles Stowe."

"Did he have a scar on his jaw?"

"Yes. Here." He points to his jaw. "You found something."

"We found his body. He was shot." She hands Marlin the spent shell.

Marlin turns it over in his hand. Bella crowds him. "Let me see that." Marlin hands it her. "It's from a pistol, a .38 revolver."

"Did you find Eleanor Blackborne?"

"No trace of her. It looks like someone came and stripped the *Ariel* and took her away with them."

"What do we do now?"

"We go find her."

Marlin shakes his head. "How are we gonna do that? There are hundreds of islands out there." He waves his arm. "And they're thousands of miles apart."

"Yes, but there aren't many white women out there." Marlin shakes his head again as he gets ready to hoist the boat on board.

DARRYL AND TANE study the western chart of the Southern Ocean. Tane points to the closest atoll.

"There are many atolls like this one with no people on them. But people go there to fish and catch turtles."

"How do you know this?"

"I go there with my father. Now I am older I go there with you."

"Set a course to the closest atoll. We'll start there and work our way through the other atolls."

As they sail west the days become hot and wet. Sometimes the wind comes from the northeast and they beat into a cross sea. They pass several small atolls and each time Darryl climbs to the crosstrees and studies them. The lagoons are empty and the strips of sand between the water and the palm trees are bare. Most of the small atolls have no pass, even for the schooner's boat. They sail on, heading slightly north until they reach Nambaten, a large atoll about five miles long. They enter the lagoon through a pass at the southeast end and anchor off a small island. The lagoon is calm, protected from the sea, but the wind blows across it, making the awning flap up and down. Most of the reef around the lagoon is awash and there are only a few islands, far apart, with one or two trees on them. No outriggers come out to meet them. They put the boat over the side and Jody and Tane go fishing. "In the morning we'll move up the lagoon."

As the sun rises Marlin raises the anchor and lets it hang from the cathead. Darryl takes the helm and sends Tane aloft to watch for coral heads. Bella has the glasses and Darryl tells her to watch the beach. "It's always possible that Mrs. Blackborne was set ashore somewhere." They sail slowly up the lagoon under main and staysail, weaving around coral heads until they reach the northern end of the atoll in the late afternoon.

Bella points toward the land. "There's a canoe with a man and a boy coming toward us."

Darryl brings the schooner into the wind, letting the sails shiver. "Marlin, let go the anchor. We'll wait for the outrigger." The crew lowers the sails as Darryl takes the glasses and studies the pass to the northeast.

The outrigger comes alongside and the man in the stern, with hair like a black haystack, grabs onto the schooner's rail. He is wearing only a loincloth and his skin is like dark leather. He stares at his feet and with his free hand pulls at his loincloth. The crew of the schooner look at him until Darryl gets a pair of pants and hands them to the man. He folds the pants carefully and lays them on his lap. The man continues to stare at his feet without saying anything until Jody gives the boy in the bow a small galley knife and then the man speaks softly, just a few words.

"He says for us to wait."

"So you can speak their language."

Tane grins. "No, but I know a little pidgin."

The man and the boy paddle back toward the land and disappear in the mangroves. An hour later a larger outrigger paddles out to the schooner with three young men. The crew of the schooner go below, looking for old pants to give them.

"Ask them about a white woman."

"You have to give them a knife, too."

"I have an old clasp knife." Marlin gives the knife to the man in the bow.

"They say go to Saway. There is a boat with two white men."

"And a white woman?"

"They do not talk about a white woman."

Darryl goes below and stands over the chart. Saway is an atoll about a day's sail to the southwest. She plots a course and returns to the deck. The outrigger with the three men is already paddling away. "Set the mainsail. We'll try the pass while it's still light."

They shorten sail in the night and in the morning the sun lights up Saway Atoll. Tane goes aloft to direct them through the pass. There's a ketch in the lagoon and Darryl brings the schooner within fifty yards of her and Marlin lets go the anchor. Darryl waves Marlin to follow her into the aft cabin.

"What are you gonna do?"

Darryl takes out the rifle. "The men on the ketch may be dangerous. I want you to cover me when I go over there."

"I don't like this. I'm not gonna use a gun."

Bella has her head in the companionway. "Give it to me. I can shoot." She climbs down the ladder and takes the rifle from Darryl. "It's a Springfield." She takes out the bolt. "And it's loaded." She looks down the barrel. "You didn't clean it, did you." She unloads the rifle, takes the cleaning kit from in the gun locker and rams a piece of cloth down the barrel.

Darryl sits in the boat and Tane rows her over to the ketch. As they approach the stern, Darry reads the name, *Sybil*. Two men in the cockpit wave them aboard and Darryl climbs up at the mizzen shrouds. The ketch was once a beautiful flush-deck yacht but now she is in poor condition, the woodwork bare and cracked and the rigging slack and the sails dark with mildew, except for a new jib furled on the bowsprit. "Good day. I'm mate of the *Eleanor Mooreland*. Captain Blackborne sent me over as a courtesy."

"Well, that's mighty fine. I'm Captain Marrow and this is my mate, Mr. Boone." Marrow has faded eyes and a scraggly beard covering most of his sunburnt face. There's a gold band on his little finger.

Darryl looks about. "Where's your crew?"

When Marrow doesn't answer, Boone starts in loud and angry. "That bastard Satini came in here and took'em, took'em all." Darryl looks from Marrow to Boone and back again. They are both worn and dirty and except for the gold ring, they look like twins.

"Don't talk, Boone."

"Well, he did. Said he was gonna double their pay, but I know for a fact he don't pay his crew hardly at all."

"That means you're stuck here?"

"Wait Boone, let me talk. No, we ain't stuck here. It doesn't take more than us two to sail *Sybil*. We've been resting up after having a touch of fever. We'd offer you a drink but we're fresh out."

"Come over to the *Ellie* and Captain Blackborne will be sure to offer you something." Darryl looks in the companionway where a gun belt is hanging on a hook. "Say, sometime in the afternoon." Darryl climbs in the boat and Tane rows her back to the schooner.

In the afternoon the captain and mate of the *Sybil* row over to the schooner. When Darryl meets them at the rail, they are both wearing gun belts. "Leave you guns in the boat."

"Nah. They'll get wet."

"Bella."

Bella comes from behind the mainmast and aims the rifle at the two men in the boat. "Do what the captain says."

Boone looks at Bella and puffs out his cheeks. "She's just a woman." Bella shoots a hole through the brim of Boone's dirty panama and the bullet strikes the water beyond the boat.

Boone grabs his hat. "Damn. Watch what you're doing."

"Do what the captain says. Drop your gun belts."

"Tane, collect the guns." Tane jumps in the boat, picks up the gun belts and throws them on the deck of the schooner. Darryl takes one of the pistols and checks that it's loaded. She waves the pistol at the two men in the dinghy. "Start rowing ashore. Bella, get in the bow of our boat and keep an eye on them. Tane, let's follow them. I have a few questions I want to ask."

When Tane beaches the boat, Marrow and Boone are still sitting in their dinghy. "Go sit on the beach and put your hands over your head."

"Why do you want us here? We can have a little talk on your schooner. You said you had something to drink. We ain't had nothing to drink for a while yet."

"You come to my schooner with guns to threaten me and my crew."

"Boone, let me talk." He turns to Darryl. "What do you want?"

"I want that ring on your little finger."

"It's stuck. I can't get it off."

"Bella."

Bella shoots the top of Marrow's ear off. Marrow cries out and claps his hand over his ear. Blood runs between his fingers.

"The ring." Marrow works on the ring, wiggling it back and forth. Blood drips from his hand and the ring slips off.

Darryl takes the ring to the edge of the water and washes off the blood. She looks inside at the engraving. *Andrew*. "Where did you get this ring?"

"I don't remember."

"Bella."

"Wait. I got it from a woman."

"What woman?"

"She was on an atoll. Her yacht was wrecked. We . . . we rescued her."

"Where is she now?"

"I don't know."

"You say 'I don't remember' or 'I don't know' one more time and Bella will shoot more than your ears

160

off." She takes a step closer. "Where is the woman now?"

Boone starts yelling. "She's on the *Black Dog*. We sold her to Captain Satini."

Darryl turns away from the two men. "Tane, tie their dinghy to our boat and row me out to the ketch. Bella, you mind staying here for a bit?"

"I like to shoot."

Darryl climbs aboard *Sybil* and goes into the aft cabin. She finds two rifles and boxes of ammunition and puts them in *Sybil's* dinghy. "There are people below. It has a lock." Tane points to the midships hatch. "I will look for a hammer."

Tane comes back with an iron bar and hits the lock until it breaks. He opens the hatch and three Islanders climb on deck. The Islanders talk quietly among themselves and then the older one addresses Tane.

"They want some water."

"Tell them to go in the aft cabin and take whatever they want." The Islanders look confused. "Tell them the other white men aren't here anymore." Tane follows the Islanders aft.

Later the Islanders return to the deck, carrying food and clothing. They look at Darryl with distrust. They are uncertain about taking things. "The older man is Makir. He is a navigator."

"Ask him if he can find his way home on this boat."

"He says he can find his way home but not on this boat. This boat is no good. He wants to go home on the schooner."

"Okay. Tell them again they can take whatever they want and then row them over to the *Ellie*. Wait. Ask him if there was a woman on the boat."

"He says yes. The white men treat her bad."

"Why were you talking about Mary?"

"It is the pidgin word for white woman." Tane rows the Islanders to the schooner and Darryl looks through the aft cabin again. There is nothing of value. She opens the seacocks in the galley and engine room. On deck she lets the anchor chain run out and watches as the bitter end slips into the water. The ketch begins to drift up the lagoon, toward the reef. Darryl climbs in *Sybil's* dinghy and rows back to the beach. She takes the pistol out of her belt and holds it to her side and walks to the two men who are now sitting under a palm tree.

"The Islanders on your ketch say you mistreated the woman."

"What's it to you?"

"The woman is why I'm here. Eleanor Blackborne is the owner of the schooner anchored in the lagoon."

"She gave us a lot of trouble."

"Did the man give you a lot of trouble too?"

They don't answer and then Boone starts yelling. "What did you do? *Sybil* is drifting toward the reef."

"I'm giving you some time to think about what it means to be rescued. Come Bella, we're going back to the *Ellie*."

"You can't leave us here like this."

"No? I don't want you to give me any trouble."

DARRYL AND BELLA return to the schooner and Bella takes all the guns to the aft cabin and starts cleaning them. Darryl sets *Sybil's* dinghy adrift and the wind sends it after the ketch. She goes to the stern and watches the ketch hit the reef. There aren't any waves to throw her onto the reef and she slowly sink as she rubs up against the corral. Marlin joins her. "Marlin, how long have you been on the *Ellie?*"

"Almost ten years, since Captain Blackborne bought her."

"You are the only experienced seaman on board and you know every inch of the schooner. The rest of us are green. I know that. But if you don't accept me as your captain, I'll take you to Deep Harbor and put you ashore."

Marlin watches *Sybil* sinking and then turns to the island. "What happened over there?"

163

Darryl holds up her right hand. "I got Eleanor Blackborne's ring."

"How do you know it's her ring?"

Darryl takes it off and hands it to Marlin. "Look inside."

Marlin looks at the ring but he is thinking of something else. "I heard a gunshot."

"Captain Marrow wouldn't tell me what I wanted to know. Bella shot his ear off. Then he told me they found Eleanor Blackborne on Epang Atoll. I think they mistreated her, at least that's what those Islanders say. Later they sold her—their words—to the captain of the schooner *Black Dog*." The hull of *Sybil* slips below the surface of the lagoon.

"Are you gonna leave them on this atoll? They'll die here."

"Captain Blackborne believed in retribution."

"Yes, he did . . . Now Captain Blackborne is dead, killed in some savage way. You left that unfinished."

"I haven't forgotten it but *Ellie* and the crew come first."

He nods but doesn't smile. "I had my doubts at first. Command is more than navigation. I guess you know that." He reaches out his hand. "Captain Simmons, I'll be here as long as you do what's right."

Darryl takes his hand. "Good. Now get the schooner underway." He goes forward. His trust is shallow but she doesn't expect more.

THE CHART SHOWS islands spread out to the west. One of them is Makir's island. Darryl plots a course and goes on deck to tell Tane to steer due west. Makir is squatting on the weather deck next to the helm staring forward. He has a high forehead and a broad nose, his brown face serious, concentrated, his beard, little more than a few hairs, is turning white.

Makir taps his right knee and Tane heads the schooner half point to starboard. "What are you two doing?"

"He sets the course to his island. He says there is a current that pushes the schooner that way." He points to the south.

"How does he know that?"

"He looks back at Saway Atoll and sees it moves the other way."

Darryl steps behind the helm and checks the compass. West-by-North. "Give me the helm, Tane, and go to the galley and bring a cup of coffee. Put a little sugar in it." Darryl waits and then very slowly steers the schooner a half point to port. Makir continues to stare forward and then taps his right knee until Darryl brings the schooner back to starboard. Tane comes aft with the coffee. "Give it to Makir."

Darryl gives Tane the helm. "What does he say?"

"He says the current runs against the waves, makes them stand up. He means makes them steep."

Darryl looks at the waves. She can't see any difference, not without a comparison. She will have to pay more attention to how the waves behave.

Makir squats next to the helm all day. In the evening the Islanders bring him food and water. When a faint star appears off the starboard bow Makir corrects the schooner's course. Darryl sits with the helmsman all night, watching Makir watch the stars as they fall toward the western horizon. The stars follow a path in the sky, one after the other, as they always have, and Makir follows their path.

The next day Tane tells Darryl how Marrow and Boone captured the Islanders. They were in their outrigger canoe repairing their sail when the *Sybil* appeared and ran them down. Marrow and Boone pulled them out of the sea and put them in the ketch's hold with other Islanders. When *Sybil* was in Saway the *Black Dog* came and Marrow let everyone out of the hold and the captain of the *Black Dog* took the boys and young men. He didn't want any old men, especially not any navigators.

Makir listens to Tane's story. Darryl is not sure how much English Makir knows but she senses that he knows some. Makir points at the sun and Tane interprets. "Makir asks why you do not look at the sun. He means why you do not use the sextant."

"Tell him, he wants to go home. I trust his navigation." Before Tane can repeat that in pidgin, Makir's expression changes slightly. It's almost a smile.

In the late afternoon Marlin complains that Makir keeps correcting his steering. "Does he even know where he is?"

Darrly looks at Makir and Makir points directly north. "Tumur, three hours."

Marlin grumbles. "I don't see anything." Darryl knows from the chart that Makir is right but she doesn't say anything. Tane goes aloft and from the crosstrees he points where Makir pointed. "There is an atoll." Marlin grumbles again. "There're a lot of atolls out here. That could be any one of them." Marlin is angry because the Islander can navigate across the open sea without compass, chart, or sextant.

WHEN THE SUN RISES they can see Rovigno Atoll and Makir gets up for the first time since coming aboard and walks forward to the other island men. "Makir says there is no place to anchor on Rovigno."

167

"We'll heave-to in the lee of the atoll and wait for them to come out in their outriggers. I'll take the helm. Go in the galley and tell Jody to make sure they are all fed. They like coffee. See that they all have a cup before they leave."

There are no outriggers in sight. Darryl scans the island with glasses: a village of huts and a big house to store canoes, no people. Tane comes aft. "Makir says he wants to go ashore."

"Okay, you and Marlin put the boat over the side. Bella, go in the aft cabin and get out a rifle but stay there."

"You think there's gonna be some trouble?"

"The people on the atoll probably think we are trouble."

Tane and the three Islanders crowd into the boat, and as Tane rows, Makir guides the boat through the surf. They drag the boat up on the beach and walk into the village. Half an hour later Makir leads a group of men to the canoe house. They sit in a circle and talk and drink and then Makir and Tane walk to the beach and Tane rows out to the schooner.

"The black schooner was here. They killed an old woman and her man when they tried to hide their son. Then they took twelve young men, mostly teen-agers."

"Where are they taking them?"

"No one knows. Makir says go to Deep Harbor and tell the commissioner what happened."

"Do any of the Islanders want to come with us?"

"No. They are afraid to go there. They get captured and taken to a plantation."

THE SCHOONER HEADS south on a close reach, making six knots. Darryl and Tane sit on the cabin top and Darryl shows him how to use the sextant. "Try it now. It's almost noon." Tane brings the sun down to the horizon and slowly adjusts the sextant as the sun continues to rise.

"The sun stopped going up."

"Read the altitude and come below."

Darryl walks Tane through the calculations. When they are finished, Tane looks up. "I don't understand everything."

"I know. Once the steps become familiar, you will learn what they mean."

Tane goes on deck to start his watch and Darryl goes into the aft cabin. She has an itch. She opens a drawer and takes out the photograph of the young woman. As she looks at it, the image of the woman slowly prints itself on her mind. She will dream of her.

The bay at Deep Harbor is wide and shallow, too shallow for a cement landing. There isn't a pier either. Everything, people, animals, and goods, need to be brought ashore in boats. Debris collects on the mud beach and on the left side of the harbor there is a maritime skid row, an array of wooden hulks rafted together and sitting in the mud at low tide. Along the waterfront are a few unpainted buildings with tin roofs and behind the buildings a green jungle grows up the side of a mountain. Clouds hang over the mountain and when it rains, water pours down the gullies and rushes toward the harbor, washing the debris away from the beach until the next tide brings it back.

Darryl sits in the stern of the boat as Tane rows her ashore. She wades through the debris and then walks up the beach, the mud sucking at her feet. "Take the boat back to the *Ellie*. I'll hail you when I'm ready to return." She uses one foot to wipe the mud off the other foot, puts on her sandals and walks toward the building with most of its paint still clinging to it. On the wall next to the door is a polished brass sign: Resident Commissioner. She opens the door and walks up to the desk. "I'm captain of the *Eleanor Mooreland*, anchored in the harbor. I want to report a crime."

Captain

The small, balding man behind the desk looks surprised. "A crime here in Deep Harbor?"

"No, on Rovigno Atoll. The schooner *Black Dog* killed two people and kidnaped twelve teenagers there."

"Wait here." The man goes into the back office. Murmuring comes through the thin walls and then the man returns. "The Assistant Commissioner will see you."

The Assistant Commissioner is sitting behind a polished mahogany desk. Behind him is a large photograph of a man in a uniform covered with medals. The Assistant Commissioner doesn't stand or extend a hand and he leaves Darryl standing before him. He has the red face of certain white men in the tropics, a redness produced from too much sun and gin. He screws up his face to look stern. A schoolmaster's face. "Let me make something clear. Captain Satini of the *Black Dog* has a license to recruit workers. This is a difficult business and Captain Satini has been very successful at it."

"Captain Satini or his men killed an older couple who were trying to protect their son."

"You saw this? No? If there are no witnesses then there is nothing to be done. You see, this happens now and then. A man puts his mark on a work contract and receives his signing bonus and then he changes his mind. He gets excited and starts shouting and then the trouble starts."

"There are laws against kidnapping."

"Of course there are laws against kidnapping but out here in the islands we have to adjusts the laws sometimes. Let me explain something to you. The development of these islands depends on two things, our financial and technical support and the Islanders' labor. This is a fair division of the responsibilities and the benefits for Islanders are substantial. Just consider for a moment, a man with a plantation can't be called a savage."

"Do Islanders own the plantations?"

"We are just beginning. You must think in terms of the future." He stops and smiles at Darryl. "Is there anything else I can do for you, Captain?"

"Do you know where Captain Satini takes his recruits?"

"There's a large sugar plantation on Takaro Island. They always need workers and they pay well for them." He smiles again. "I have heard that Captain Satini does not like to be interfered with."

Darryl considers the red face for a moment. "Of course not. I don't either."

Captain

THE SCHOONER HEADS south again and the wind whips spray over the bow and wets the foredeck. Darryl waits for a cloud to pass and then she takes the morning sun sight. Later she watches Tane take the noon sight. She checks Tane's calculations. They should sight Takaro Island tomorrow. She goes back on deck and sits next to Bella at the helm. Bella is comfortable standing watch now. She sits at the helm humming, as the wind tangles her hair.

"Did you help Jody make the fish casserole this morning?"

"He has never made one before." She looks at Darryl. "I don't mind working in the galley as long as it's not my job."

"That's okay. Jody likes working in the galley, as long as he has fresh air. Go eat with the others. I'll take the helm." When Bella returns, Darryl goes forward and eats standing in the galley and then helps Jody clean up. The afternoon is quiet as the schooner pitches into the sea, sending spray back to the fore mast. Darryl goes into the aft cabin and takes out the photograph of the young woman. She stares at the photograph as if it will help her find Eleanor Blackborne.

They heave-to off Takaro Island and after the crew eats breakfast they get underway again. Darryl can see the pass but there are waves breaking inside the lagoon. She sends Tane aloft with the glasses. She can't see anything on the island. The lagoon is large and extends more than a mile from the barrier reef. Tane returns to the deck. "Many reefs and corral heads inside. There are some signs painted white."

Darryl takes the glasses. "Those are range markers. Line them up, one above the other, and they lead us into the channel." Water washes over corral heads in the lagoon. Some of them have poles with wicker baskets on them to mark their location. They anchor off a cement landing and before they have cleared the deck, a boat comes out from the shore with two Islanders rowing and a white man sitting in the stern.

"Ahoy, may I come aboard?" The Islanders stay in the boat as the tall white man with a drooping mustache and clean but wrinkled clothes climbs aboard and approaches Marlin. "Hullo. I'm George Kaine. I run the station here." He waves a thin arm at the island and smiles faintly. There isn't much to see. A house with a veranda and some cleared land behind it. The plantation is probably farther back.

"Name's Marlin."

Kaine looks around. "Well, Captain Marlin, I see you haven't brought me any workers?"

"We don't recruit." Darryl, standing behind Kaine, pantomimes taking a drink. Marlin smiles. "But we can give you a drink."

"Yes, yes, please do."

"Bella, I think there's some rum in the aft cabin. Why don't you get a bottle." Marlin leads Kaine down to the saloon and when Bella arrives he pours Kaine a glass of rum and then another glass for himself.

"We don't get much rum out here, mostly it is gin." Kaine takes the glass in his long fingers and holds it up to the light. "This has a nice color." He takes a sip. "I am surprised to see you. I don't get many visitors and now I've had two almost at the same time." He takes another sip. "This is very good. Yes, Captain Satini was here, brought me some workers a few days ago, young men. They make good workers. They spend three years working on the plantation and at the end of their time I pay them off, usually in trade goods, and they go home and pick any woman they want as a wife. Working here really sets them up."

Before Darryl can stop him, Tane breaks in. "Do all the workers go home?"

"Well, some are in debt. You see they buy too much on credit at the station store, tobacco mostly, and they have to work that off. And some of them break the law and they cannot go home until the end of their sentence." He takes a sip. "Yes, sometimes they run away. That is a violation of their contract and an important part of our responsibility here is teaching them to respect the law."

Darryl shakes her head at Tane. "When did you say Captain Satini left here?"

"Have I said?" He wipes his mustache with his hand. "Yes, he left yesterday. Maybe you saw him on your way in. He spent a few days here, waiting for his mate to sharpen a boathook on my grindstone." Kaine holds his glass up again. "This is excellent." As he drinks his face begins to turn pink.

Marlin holds up his glass. "Down the hatch."

"Yes, Captain Satini can be very amusing. He told me he has caught everything, man and beast, except a whale. He said he wants to use the boathook as a harpoon." He smiles. "Captain Satini is a good businessman but even a businessman has to take his fun now and then."

Marlin takes a sip. "Do you know where Satini and the *Black Dog* are headed?"

"Right. He is captain of the *Black Dog*. She is even painted black. Satini said he is going up to Fanagoon. Do you know it? It is a big atoll up north of here. The recruiting there used to be good until last year when the *Don Juan* was attacked in the lagoon. The kanakas got hundreds of canoes together and surrounded her and overran everything. The people on *Don Juan* didn't stand a chance, even with rifles. Only a few of her kanaka crew survived."

"We are looking for someone. She may be on *Black Dog*. Did you go aboard the schooner while she was here?"

"Now that is a strange question. No, he did not let me on aboard. He said some of his people were sick but I hardly believe that. None of the workers he brought me are sick." He takes a sip. "Yes, I guess he will stop at Deep Harbor on the way north. He is short of crew and he can usually pick up a few kanakas there." Darryl nods at Tane and Bella and they get up and go on deck. "You think you can catch up with him? I have a feeling he will not like that."

"Mr. Kaine, finish your drink. We are getting underway in fifteen minutes." Kaine's eys widen as he looks at Darryl.

THE RAIN BRINGS mist down from the mountain and obscures the bay at Deep Harbor. The schooner is hove-to off the pass and Darryl stands at the helm in an oilskin as the crew eats lunch below. Rain drips under her collar and spreads down her back. She will go below when the mist clears. Two bells sound. Tane comes on deck, looks at Darryl and climbs aloft. He returns to the deck and walks aft. "No boats in the harbor. Only those old wrecks tied together." Darryl goes below for the glasses and then climbs aloft to the crosstrees. The rain has almost stopped and the mist is beginning to clear. Tane is right. There is nothing in the harbor. Of course, it would have been too easy to catch *Black Dog* here. She climbs down and sets a course for Fanagoon Atoll.

AT THE END of the last dog watch Marlin goes forward and Tane takes the helm. Darryl likes to be on deck when the watch changes. She sits on the steering box and looks at the sun sinking toward the horizon. The western sky turns red and although the wind hasn't changed, the evening feels gentler. A water spout sprays the face of the sun, as if to help end the day. "Look. A whale is blowing." The massive head dives and the flukes rise up and slide into the sea. "That's the first whale I've seen."

"I hear them at night sometimes. They come close to greet us."

"You've never written that in the log."

"You said write if something is unusual."

In the morning they are close to Fanagoon Atoll but they can't see it yet. A squall comes up from behind and the wind and rain whips them across the sea. Everyone is wet and it's cold but refreshing. When the horizon clears they see *Black Dog* outlined against the atoll, black and low, her two masts truncated. "She's not carrying topmasts." Darryl raises the glasses. Something is wrong. She is hove-to under foresail, drifting parallel to the barrier reef of the atoll.

"Bella, I'm going aboard *Black Dog*. If there is any trouble, fire a round over their heads."

"And if it doesn't stop them?" The two women look at each other until Bella smiles. "I know what to do."

They heave-to up wind and Tane rows as Darryl studies *Black Dog,* trying to see why she is hove-to so close to the reef. "When I go aboard, stay in the boat and keep it ready to shove off." Tane rows up to the weather side, just below the main shrouds. "Ahoy, permission to board."

A white man with a carefully trimmed beard looks over the side. His black hair is short and his eyes are a piercing green that makes Darryl stare and then look away. "Have you come to lend me a hand?"

Darryl leaps for the shrouds and climbs aboard. Two bodies hang from the fore crosstrees, one on each side of the mast. "It looks like you have the situation under control."

The man is small and carefully dressed in white, including his shoes, giving an impression of fastidiousness. "My steering gear is jammed and a few of the kanakas tried to take advantage of the situation. I am Captain Satini. What schooner is that? "

"The *Eleanor Mooreland.*"

"I have not heard of you before. Are you recruiting workers?"

"No, it's a pleasure cruise. The owner is collecting island artifacts."

"I see. Let me offer you a drink." Darryl follows Satini into the aft cabin.

"Do you need some help with your steering gear?"

"You may not believe this but we were attacked by a whale. As it approached us, I threw a harpoon and hit it just behind the spout. It was an excellent throw but it confused the whale and instead of running away so I could give chase, it rammed our rudder and broke the steering gear. My mate is trying to jury-rig it now." He holds up his white hands. "As you can see, I am a gentleman." He smiles with his lips closed and rests his right hand on the handle of the revolver in his gun belt. "My task is to maintain discipline."

"We have an engineer on board. He's rather talented. I can bring him over and he can have a look at your steering gear."

"Excellent. Perhaps we could do that now and postpone the drink until later."

As Satini turns toward the companionway, a door opens at the other end of the cabin and Eleanor Blackborne steps in, barefoot, wearing a white linen dress. She is pale as if she has been avoiding the sun.

"You were to remain in your cabin."

Eleanor ignores Satini's irritable tone. "It's stifling in there. It's always stifling when we aren't sailing." She steps forward with an outstretched hand. "I'm Eleanor Blackborne." Darryl is wearing Eleanor's ring and as Eleanor holds Darryl's hand, she turns it to look at the ring.

"Darryl Simmons."

"Mrs. Blackborne is my guest. She suffers from a nervous disorder and is cruising with me for her health."

"Yes, Captain Satini has been very kind and patient with me, going out of his way to show me some very remote atolls."

"Mr. Simmons is going to helps us with that wretched steering gear. Come, Mr. Simmons, the sooner we can get *Black Dog* underway again, the better Mrs. Blackborne will feel."

"I feel fine." Eleanor follows Satini and Darryl as they climb on deck. Darryl wonders what the two of them are like when she isn't there.

"You know you should stay below."

"I feel fine. The fresh sea air does me good. You are always saying that."

Satini looks to windward and then at the reef. "The wind is backing." He hesitates. "Mr. Buncombe!" A white man in dirty clothes climbs out of a small hatch over the lazaret. "Get the longboat over the side and start towing the schooner. You see." He points at the reef. Darryl climbs in her boat and Satini calls after her. "Ask your captain to give as a tow."

Darryl waves to him. "We'll be with you in no time." She turns to Tane. "Shove off." Tane stares at her because she is still holding onto the rail of the *Black Dog*.

Satini starts forward to where his crew is getting the long boat ready to hoist. "Quick now. Jump." Eleanor climbs over the rail and leaps into the boat, falling at Darryl's feet. Darryl pushes the boat away from the schooner. "Give way! Give way!" Tane grunts as he rises off the thwart with each stroke of the oars.

Eleanor lies huddled in the bottom of the boat and Darryl puts a hand on her back to keep her from rising. Satini steps back to the main shrouds and shouts after them. "Hold." He draws his pistol. "Hold, now." A gunshot. A piece of wood flies off *Black Dog's* mainmast near Satini's head and he withdraws to the lee side of his schooner.

"Is he shooting at us?"

"No. That was from us. We're safe now."

Eleanor sits up in the bottom of the boat and looks about. "When I heard *Eleanor Mooreland* was in Deep Harbor I knew Andrew would find me."

"I found you."

"You? Where is Andrew?"

"He's at Manulele Atoll."

When they reach the schooner Marlin meets them at the main shrouds and helps Eleanor climb aboard. "How are you Mrs. Blackborne. We are very glad to see you." Darryl can tell from Marlin's face that she won't be having any more trouble from him.

THE CREW OF THE *BLACK DOG* get their longboat in the water and start towing the schooner away from the reef but they are making little headway against the wind.

"That schooner is gonna end up on the reef if we don't help her."

"Marlin, get the glasses and look at what's hanging from their foremast, then get the boat on board."

Darryl follows Eleanor into the aft cabin. "This is still Andrew's cabin."

"Yes." Even in the dim cabin light Darryl can see Eleanor's gray eyes and light brown hair, colors that the black-and-white photograph only hinted at.

"Why are you staring at me?"

"You are so young, almost as young as I am."

"Yes, Andrew likes young women." She looks carefully at Darryl. "You aren't his type. You aren't pretty enough." She runs her hand through her hair. "Do you have a brush?" Darryl gets a brush from above her bunk. Eleanor begins brushing her hair while looking at Darryl. "Andrew taught you to sail? He likes to teach. That's why I left him. I wanted a lover not a teacher. What is Andrew doing on an atoll?"

"He's buried there."

She stops brushing. "I guess I am sorry . . . Tell me what happened later and I will go there, but first I want to know what is going to happen to the *Black Dog*."

"There's a good chance she'll end up on the reef."

"Tell Marlin I want to watch."

"Mrs. Blackborne. I am the captain."

"I see." She smiles. "Call me Nora."

Captain

Darryl and Eleanor watch as the wind drives the *Black Dog* toward the reef. A squall sweeps across the sea to leeward and the *Black Dog* disappears in the mist and rain. When the sky clears the *Black Dog* is lying on the edge of reef, rising and falling as waves break over her. Tane climbs down from aloft, glasses around his neck. "The people have left the schooner. They are in the long boat."

"Where are they going?"

"They go to the lagoon."

"I want to follow them."

Faragoon Atoll is a large oval, ten miles from end to end, with only a few breaks in the strip of land that surrounds the lagoon. Darryl sends Tane aloft again and heads the schooner up the side of the atoll. As they approach the pass, Eleanor points to it. "Take the schooner into the lagoon."

"No, ma'am. The Islanders don't know we are friendly. They will swarm us with their canoes and take over the schooner."

Eleanor turns to Marlin. "What do you think?"

"Mrs. Blackborne, I didn't think it was possible, but Captain Simmons found you. I would listen to him."

"You call her him?"

"Yes ma'am. She's a him."

They hear gunfire from farther up the atoll. Tane calls down from the crosstrees. "The people are attacking the longboat." He is pointing but from the deck they can see only palm trees. Eleanor jumps into the main shrouds and climbs to the crosstrees. When the gunfire stops she returns to the deck, grim but satisfied.

Tane reaches the deck and walks aft. "The people have the longboat. I think they killed the white men."

Darryl follows Eleanor into the aft cabin. "It's over. Have you seen enough?"

"Yes." Darryl doesn't move. "What is it?"

"As long as I am the captain, the schooner and her crew come first. If you are dissatisfied with me, you'll have to wait until we are in port to dismiss me."

"I have no intention of dismissing you."

"Then do not question my authority in front of the crew."

"You make us sound like we are two squabbling women."

"Squabbling women is something I want to avoid, so I have one more request. The crew doesn't like having two bosses. You order me and let me order the crew."

"That will do as long as you obey me."

"You are the owner."

"Good. Is there something to drink on board"

Darryl points. "In that locker there is some rum."

Eleanor takes out a bottle and pours rum in two glasses and hands a glass to Darryl. "What do you know about Captain Marrow and his mate Boone?"

Darryl takes the ring from her finger. "I found this on Captain Boone. Eventually it led me to you. You want to go to Saway Atoll?"

"So you've met Captain Marrow and Boone. Are they still there?"

"I left them there."

Eleanor considers Darryl. "I'm not sure what that means but if they are still on the atoll then I want to go there. They—"

"Sold you to Satini. I'll set the course."

THEY SAIL EAST with the wind forward of the beam. A line of squalls covers the southern horizon but the weather is generally good. Tane takes the morning as well as the noon sight, and watching him, Darryl thinks he has the sea in his genes because he learns faster than she does. She goes into the aft cabin where Eleanor is in the port bunk reading. "Can I ask you something." She gets out the photograph of the young woman. "How old were you when this photo was taken?"

"That was before I met Andrew. He saw the photo and wanted it."

"Why did you marry him?"

Eleanor raises her eyebrows. "He named his schooner after me." She sits up. "And he was very persuasive."

"And then you left him."

"I told you about that. Andrew wasn't gentle. Don't make a face. You know the gods aren't gentle. But a woman like me expects it." She studies Darryl. "You aren't gentle either, kind maybe, but not gentle."

As they approach the pass at Saway, Darryl points out the tops of *Sybil's* masts rising out of the lagoon. It's shallow there or the ketch is resting on a corral shelve. Darryl rows Eleanor ashore, leaving the crew on the schooner. They walk along the beach, looking for signs of the two men Darryl left on the atoll. When they don't find anything, they walk in under the palm trees. There is a rotten smell, very faint. The two men are in a grove of palms with their backs leaning against trees, their eyes gone along with most of the flesh on their faces. The crabs and the birds. They sit there facing each other, grinning with black teeth. Darryl can't tell them apart.

Eleanor stares at the two corpses. "You did this."

"I did what Captain Blackborne would have done."

"You think you know him better than me? Is that what you want to say?"

"Why are we here? You wanted to see what happened to them. You wanted retribution for what these men did to you."

"They didn't mistreat me, if that is what you mean. They were always too drunk. But you didn't answer me."

"What about Captain Satini? He just wanted to show you remote atolls?"

"He thought too much of himself to force himself on me. But you still didn't answer me. You think you know Andrew better than me?"

"What does it matter? No, I don't know him better. Remember, I'm not his type. I'm not pretty, just loyal."

They walks back to the beach and Darryl rows out to the schooner. She doesn't like arguing with Eleanor but she doesn't know how to avoid it. Eleanor leans over and touches Darryl's knee. "You know, sometimes you are beautiful but it's something a man wouldn't notice."

The sun reaches the western horizon and shadows move across the lagoon. There's a moon and it lights up the whiteness of the waves breaking on the reef. It also marks the pass even after the sun is down. Darryl comes out of the chart room. "Where is Tane?" Marlin points to the engine room. "As soon as he starts the engine we get underway." She goes into the aft cabin. "We are leaving in a few minutes. Do you want to go to Epang Atoll?"

"That's where *Ariel* is. Yes, I want to go there."

"Giles is buried there."

"Yes, my whole past is buried on these islands."

THE DAY IS GRAY and the sea is rough as they heave-to off of Epang Atoll. Eleanor needs help getting into the boat as it rises and falls next to the schooner. Darryl rows Eleanor through the narrow pass and into the lagoon. The beach, the palms, and the sloop on the crushed corral, nothing has changed. Eleanor walks slowly around *Ariel*. "It was such a feeling of freedom sailing across the ocean. The days and the sea seemed endless. And then the storm caught us and threw the sloop on the beach and we were trapped here." She talks mainly to herself. She turns to Darryl. "Do you know where Giles is?"

"This way." They walk into the trees. Like the sloop, the grave hasn't changed.

Eleanor squats down and studies the coral mound. "You never asked me how he died."

"I know how he died."

She looks up. "You uncovered his body?"

"I had to know."

"You think I abandoned a great man for this poor man here. He was only Andrew's mate."

"I don't know. I never met Giles. If he was Captain Blackborne's mate then I think we must have been alike in some way."

"You assume too much." Eleanor stands and looks directly at Darryl. "You found something in Andrew that I didn't."

"No. That's not right. I just wanted something different. I wanted to know the sea and I accepted him as my mentor. I didn't want him as a lover."

"Are you saying you aren't a woman? Is that why you dress as a man?"

"I dress as a man because I get more respect. I don't want to be known as a woman-captain. It's like being called a sea-witch, or worse. You see, there is no such thing as a man-captain. There are only captains. That's the tradition of the sea."

"I think I have found you out." She smiles. "You are afraid of love."

"You have only found that I'm not like you."

"No, you are like Andrew." She turns and walks away. "Come. I have another grave to visit."

Darryl rows Eleanor back across the lagoon. She sees Eleanor sitting in the stern, facing her, but she isn't thinking of her. She's thinking of the wrecks spread across the Southern Ocean. *Tantra, Ariel, Sybil, Black Dog.* She looks over her shoulder as she rows. She doesn't want *Eleanor Mooreland* to be one of them.

THEY SIGHT MANULELE Atoll just before sundown, as red clouds light up the western sky. They approach the reef until they can see the white surf and then they heave-to and wait for dawn.

There are Islanders on the beach as the schooner enters the pass in the morning but they soon retreat back into the trees. Darryl smiles. They didn't expect to see us again. "Marlin, I'm taking Mrs. Blackborne ashore. Keep an armed watch on the schooner. I don't think we'll have any trouble during the day, but they'll be watching us and I want them to know we are watching them."

They put the boat over the side and Eleanor climbs in. "Bella, get a rifle and come with us."

Darryl rows up the lagoon to the northern end of the beach and lets the boat slide onto the sand below the graves. "Bella, stay near the boat. If any young men approach, warn them off."

Darryl leads Eleanor to the graves. "Captain Blackborne's grave is the large one. We made a coffin for him."

"Whose are these other graves?"

"Captain and mate of the schooner *Tantra*." Darryl points to what is left of the schooner on the reef. "She was wrecked in the same storm that threw *Ariel* on the beach. The storm cut a wide path through the islands."

Eleanor isn't listening. She is looking at Blackborne's grave. "You have not told me how he died?"

"You haven't asked. He was hit on the back of the head with something blunt, like a war club. It crushed his skull."

Eleanor looks up. "What have you done about this?"

"So far, nothing. That's why I am here. When you are ready, I want to talk to the priest." Eleanor turns to the beach. "Wait." Darryl bends down and retrieves Blackborne's ring. "You should have this." Eleanor takes the ring and closes her fist on it as they head back to the boat.

Darryl rows down the lagoon and beaches the boat opposite the schooner. She avoids the village as she leads Eleanor and Bella to the church. "Bella, wait outside."

Father Losefe is in the back of the church lying on a cot. He gets up and straightens his cossack. "I am surprised to see you."

"Father, I want to make a donation to your church. Here, please take this coin." Darryl hands him a twenty-dollar gold piece.

The priest holds the coin up, appraising it. "This is very generous. May I ask what has brought this on?"

"Tell the elders that I want to talk to them about taking their copra to Newtown."

"They will be pleased to hear that. The copra shed is full. We can have a meeting after services tomorrow." He smiles shyly. "I was just thinking about my sermon when you came in the church."

Eleanor asks him what he talks about to the people here.

"I will give a sermon on Cain and Able. Do you know the story? It is about a man who kills another man."

"They were brothers."

"All men are brothers. The murderer was then banished to the land of Nod, east of Eden."

"Well, he wasn't actually banished."

"I tell the story that way."

Captain

DARRYL ROWS BACK to the schooner and gathers the crew in the saloon. "We will probably be attacked tonight. I want to be ready. There will be a moon and as soon as we see men gathering at their outriggers, we will surprise them." She looks around the table.

"What if they attack us anyway, after being surprised?"

"Jody, we have five guns, three rifles and two pistols. When we fire a volley over their heads, I'm pretty sure they will run away." She smiles at them. "We'll be up late, so try to get some rest now. I'll watch this afternoon."

Eleanor joins Darryl on deck and they sit on the cabin top under the awning. "Tell me your plan."

"I think there are two factions on the island. One is Masina and Rangi and the young men, and the other is the elders and the rest of the village, the women and children. I want to discredit Masina and Rangi, so that the elders act against them."

"How will this find who murdered Andrew?"

"Everyone knows who the murderer is. The problem is turning the island against him."

"What happens then?"

"I'm not sure but when I tell the elders I will take their copra to Newtown they may exile Masina and Rangi."

"Banish them to the land of Nod?" Eleanor is smiling.

"Father Losefe's sermon my help us." Darryl points to the east. "You can't see it from here but there's a small uninhabited atoll there. It is called Nott.

When the sun goes down the half-moon shines a pale light on the atoll. The crew of the schooner drink coffee and watch the beach. Shadows begin to move under the palm trees and when Darryl sees men dragging outriggers out from under the trees, she sounds the air foghorn. The horn is louder than she remembers and everyone on board the schooner jumps. She then fires an illumination flare. As the parachute slowly descends, the men on the beach freeze in the unexpected light. "Fire your guns. Don't aim toward the village." The rifles and pistols make a ragged volley. Darryl points out Rangi. "Bella, make him feel your bullet go by. Bella aims and fires and Rangi bends over and grabs his face. "Did you hit him?"

"Nah. I shot the canoe next to him. He got some splinters in his face." The light of the flare dies out and Darryl fires another one. The beach is now empty except for the abandoned outriggers. "We'll set a watch just in case. Bella, you take the first watch. The rest of you go below. Only night lights from now on."

Captain

Darryl follows Eleanor into the aft cabin where they are two shadows in the dim light. "That was exciting. I won't be able to sleep now. What are you going to do."

Darryl moves close to Eleanor. "I'll stay with you."

"I don't want you to." She puts her hand on Darryl's cheek. "Don't look at me like that . . . We can't even be friends. You let people underestimate you. That makes you dangerous.

WHEN THE AFTERNOON SUN reaches the tops of the palm trees, Tane rows Darryl ashore and they walk to the village. The three elders, old men with fading tattoos on lose skin, sit erect at the far end of the fire pit. Their faces are impassive as they watch Darryl and Tane arrive. Masina and Rangi aren't there.

"I have come to help you with your copra. I will take it to Newtown for a good price, a better price than the trader gave you."

The elder in the middle talks, looking at Tane. "He says you want something."

"A man was murdered on this island and the murderer is still here among you. This is an evil, an evil that spreads into everything it touches. I don't want to bring this evil on my schooner with the copra."

197

The elders begin to talk among themselves. "Tane, you stay here and tell me later what they decide."

Late at night Tane hails the schooner and Darryl rows ashore. They stand on the beach and talk as a cloud passes in front of the moon.

"The elders called for the priest to tell the story of Cain and Able again. Then they discussed if an island man can be the brother of a white man, especially a white man that he hates. But in the end this is not important. They know who the murderer is, everyone knows, and they have banished Rangi to Nott Atoll. This is cruel. No one lives there. It is without water."

"And Masina?"

"They did not speak of her."

Tane rows them back to the schooner and Darryl looks in the aft cabin. Eleanor is asleep.

In the morning the entire village gathers on the beach. Tane rows Darryl and Eleanor ashore. There is a single outrigger at the edge of the water. The villagers are quiet as they wait. No one is wearing flowers. Rangi appears carrying a basket, his face blank, his anger and fierceness gone. Exile has already broken him. Behind him walks the big Islander, the one who carried the dead boar. Rangi pushes the outrigger into the lagoon and climbs aboard. He paddles out to the pass and into the sea and then sets his sail. The outrigger gathers speed and flies across the waves toward Nott Atoll. Everyone watches until he disappears below the horizon.

Masina leaves the crowd and walks to Eleanor. "You are Mrs. Blackborne. I want to go with you. My people no longer listen to me. I am not wanted here." Darryl has forgotten how beautiful Masina is, even more beautiful now than before. There is something in her face, a glow that gives her expression a surprising depth.

Eleanor turns to Darryl, her face a question. Darryl puts her hand on Masina's arm. "This is Masina, Rangi's cousin."

There are tears running down Masina's face. Eleanor steps up to her and embraces her. Time passes as the two women hold each other. Eleanor steps back and takes both of Masina's hands. "Yes, come with me. Darryl, row us out to the schooner."

Eleanor and Masina go in the aft cabin and Darryl brings them tea and slices of cornbread that Jody baked. She doesn't mind serving them, she doesn't even notice that she is doing it. She wants to know what is happening. Then Tane calls her. The Islanders are bringing the copra to the schooner.

THEY SET SAIL for Newtown and Darryl watches the aft cabin but the two women don't come out. Darryl feels excluded. As long as she was searching for Eleanor, the captain was there, in her mind guiding her, showing her the way forward, but now he is gone and Eleanor is there instead. She feels bound to Eleanor. She wants to be near her. She doesn't want love, though she would like to hold Eleanor, if only for a moment. No, it's not love. She wants what the captain gave her. She wants recognition.

After a few days the schooner powers up the narrow passage at Newtown and anchors off the pier. Eleanor comes on deck. "Darryl, we want to go ashore."

"When are you coming back?"

"We aren't coming back. Masina is pregnant and I'm taking her home. I feel responsible for her and I want to help raise the child."

"I can take you home in the schooner."

"No. I've seen enough of the Southern Ocean and the schooner reminds me too much of Andrew, of my old life with him. I want to forget that. I want to forget Andrew and Giles and everything that has happened here."

This doesn't feel right. "How can you take Masina away from here? The islands are her home."

"They're more your home now. I promised Masina that you will help her people, that you will use the *Ellie* to carry their copra, at least until someone can take your place . . . Do you want to talk to Masina?"

"No. I have nothing to say to her."

"After all that has happened you are still angry with her?" She smiles at Darryl. "You are hiding a woman's jealous heart in those man's clothes of yours."

Masina comes on deck and looks at the two other women. "Can we go now?" Her face glows and when she turns to Darryl she quickly lowers her eyes.

The boat is put over the side and Tane rows Eleanor and Masina ashore. They walk down the pier carrying small bags and disappear in the traffic on the street. For a moment Darryl doesn't move. Eleanor wants to forget everything? Including what Darryl has done for her? . . . No, not done for her. Darryl did it for herself. She's that selfish, like the captain, like he would have done.

The wind blows down from the mountains and the schooner swing at her anchor to meet it. Darryl turns to the wind, thinking of the days ahead, the simple tasks of sailing between the islands and atolls. There's still a lot to learn but there's nothing to decide now, except maybe what to do with the aft cabin. Maybe she'll move her kit there and use it from now on. She goes below. On the vanity is Blackborne's gold ring resting on a sheet of paper. "He taught you well. Nora"

When Tane returns with the boat, she calls him aft. "Mr. Palamo, I'm promoting you to mate. Move your kit aft to the chart room." Her voice is louder than she intends. "Then get the schooner up to the pier. I want the copra unloaded before noon." Marlin and Bella stop what they are doing and look at her. Her voice has never been so sharp. Darryl turns to them and smiles. "If you please."